P9-DHN-268

NOMOS
GLASHÜTTE
neomatik
MADE IN GERMANY

GRANTA

12 Addison Avenue, London W11 4QR | email: editorial@granta.com
To subscribe go to granta.com, or call 020 8955 7011 (free phone 0500 004 033)
in the United Kingdom, 845-267-3031 (toll-free 866-438-6150) in the United States

ISSUE 140: SUMMER 2017

Granta, ISSN 173231, is published four times a year by Granta Publications, 12 Addison Avenue, London W11 4QR, United Kingdom.

The US annual subscription price is $48. Airfreight and mailing in the USA by agent named Air Business Ltd, c/o Worldnet-Shipping USA Inc., 156–15 146th Avenue, 2nd Floor, Jamaica, NY 11434, USA. Periodicals postage paid at Jamaica, NY 11431.

US Postmaster: Send address changes to *Granta*, Air Business Ltd, c/o Worldnet-Shipping USA Inc., 156–15 146th Avenue, 2nd Floor, Jamaica, NY 11434, USA.

Subscription records are maintained at *Granta*, c/o Abacus e-Media, Chancery Exchange, 10 Furnival Street, London EC4A 1YH.

Air Business Ltd is acting as our mailing agent.

Granta is printed and bound in Italy by Legoprint. This magazine is printed on paper that fulfils the criteria for 'Paper for permanent document' according to ISO 9706 and the American Library Standard ANSI/NIZO Z39.48-1992 and has been certified by the Forest Stewardship Council (FSC). *Granta* is indexed in the American Humanities Index.

ISBN 978-1-909-889-08-8

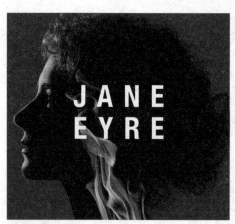

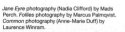

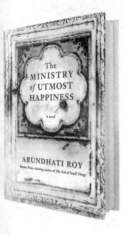

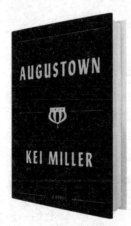

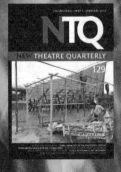

CONTENTS

Introduction

What's in a state of mind? How do we describe emotions, or the complex relationship between individuals and the state? What did Barry Lopez feel about diving under the ice in Antarctica? What caused the seemingly telepathic communication between Siri Hustvedt and her husband, Paul Auster? What happened in Max Porter's therapy session with his brother? Those are some of the short pieces in this issue – we titled the series 'State of Mind', and asked a number of writers to contribute. There are sadder moments too, some more elusive than others. Mary Ruefle thinks of names; Marcel Proust longs for silence; Margo Jefferson resists her inner voice whispering defeatist messages; Andrew Solomon meditates on gay identity and depression; and Han Kang describes her baby sister, who was born prematurely, and died long before Kang was born: 'a girl, with a face as white as a crescent-moon rice cake.'

Our lead piece, 'Notes on a Suicide', by Rana Dasgupta, delves into the mystery of Océane, the young Frenchwoman from the outskirts of Paris, Polish-Turkish by origin, who live-streamed her suicide on Periscope, a social media platform. Who was Océane, and what can her life and death tell us about the state of France? She was nineteen when she died – a girl of some talent who had imbibed the ennui of the French cultural tradition; a girl estranged from her father; a girl who had been beaten and raped by a former boyfriend. For Océane, that act of violence was too much – she had, it seems, nothing left to bind her to this world. But her public act of self-destruction was also aligned with the cultural logic of the environment she lived in, the banlieues, a space of male violence and petty degradations, of youth unemployment, graffiti and tattoos. And add to this the virtual world, a new dimension distorting and enhancing reality; add, too, ancient cults of death merging with the cult of celebrity, and the act of Océane – who is still there, on YouTube, pink hearts floating up from the bottom of the screen as she speaks, cigarette in hand – begins to make a disturbing kind of sense.

Jack Shenker lived in Cairo for many years, researching his book on Egypt. His evocative piece in this issue is about the aftermath of the revolution, the current repression that has seen scores of human rights activists jailed or disappeared, and many others going into exile. Shenker shows the reality behind words like 'political repression' – people tell him of hanging naked from their hands and feet; about suffering electric torture; about negotiating floor space in an overcrowded cell. The holes and crevices in the walls and bridges become a symbol in this text, standing for the anarchy and creativity of the revolution, in contrast to New Cairo, the sterile government suburb erected on the banks of the Nile, far away from the life of the inner city.

Charles Glass and Don McCullin, travelling in the Kurdistan Regional Governorate in Iraq, found an ISIS fighter in custody. As a teenager with al-Qaeda, Ali Qahtan kidnapped and killed policemen; with ISIS, he killed Kurdish fighters. He now expresses remorse. Was he tortured? Glass asks. For the first time, Qahtan makes eye contact, and answers, emphatically, yes. He is not allowed to say more – it is an operational matter, the Kurdish intelligence officer says, briefly.

Don McCullin's photograph is dense and bleak, showing a young man leaning slightly forward, handcuffed. He has killed many people, and betrayed his ISIS comrades too, who were subsequently arrested. A man sits behind a desk across from him – the Kurdish jailer I thought at first, impressed by his humane demeanour, then I look more closely and see that it's Charles Glass himself. Here he is, with a man who embodies the enemy of the West, a known killer. And here he is, with an ordinary guy in a black jacket, anxious and defeated.

We think they are one thing, and then suddenly they become another. ■

Sigrid Rausing

Anubis, Egyptian god of the dead, mummification, and the afterlife, *c*. 330 BCE
Courtesy of the Metropolitan Museum of Art, New York

NOTES ON A SUICIDE

Rana Dasgupta

'Quand j'partirai ne venez pas pleurer sur ma tombe.
Combien sont sincères?'

(When I've gone, don't come and weep on my grave.
How many are sincere?)
– La Fouine

1

Until the 1960s – when the new world turned resentfully on the old – the river-wrinkled region to the south of Paris was dotted with handsome country towns made modern by the railways.

Many of the brave stations and postal depots from that era have since fallen into decrepitude, but they still hold the memory of the erstwhile alchemy. Twin rails conducted industrial vigour into the most rustic of locales: the *espresso* (for it was the Italians who expressed it, collapsing caffeine and locomotives into one steam-powered word) of economic expansion and minute-precision time. Suddenly, provincial farmers could send perishable produce to

Paris, where, a mere two hours out of the ground, it would sell for metropolitan prices in the crammed stalls of Les Halles. But they were simultaneously engulfed by the greater force of the city moving out to them: for industrialists, too, could propel products far afield on the railways, so why not manufacture them outside the capital, where land and labour were cheap?

There was the town of Arpajon, for instance, whose fruit and vegetables were so urgently needed in Les Halles that a thirty-seven-kilometre railway was built to link them door-to-door. But the town's population was also swelling with the influx of new enterprises: breweries and tanneries, and especially the shoe factory, set up in 1859. All this created a new bourgeoisie who built large homes in a self-sufficiently regional style: coated with rough-hewn stone, colourfully painted on the lintels, stretching unnaturally thin and tall. There were parks laid out, and pretty streets of shops, and a grandiose city hall. The railway station – source of everything – was appropriately imposing.

The same rule is shown by its exceptions: take the nearby village of Grigny, which the railway lines did not touch, and which maintained, therefore, an older sense of time. It became bucolic: horse-drawn carts took Parisian day trippers from the nearest station to sit in Grigny's tourist pavilions, where they could breathe invigorating country air and draw nourishment from the prospect of gently rolling hills. The pastoral eternity of this view was made poignant, all the same, by a modern frisson: sweeping past the distant peasants labouring in the grain fields was the stern line of the Vanne aqueduct – erected as part of Baron Georges-Eugène Haussmann's re-engineering of the capital in the 1860s – which filled greedy Parisian reservoirs with pure water captured 200 kilometres away.

Today, Grigny is a grimy assemblage of 1970s housing blocks. New facades on the schools fly the flags of France and the European Union, and are painted with edifying quotations from great white men, but they are masks for falling-down classrooms. Doctors do not want to work there, and the lone public health centre is always on the brink of closure, even though Grigny plays host to some of France's most florid health problems – a veritable epidemic of HIV-induced chronic diseases among women, for instance. Half the young are poor and have nothing to do, and the vacuum is often filled with drugs and petty crime. The cost of preventing theft recently drove away Grigny's only supermarket, the great shell of which now lies empty; in other stores the shelves are roped off from customers, who must ask staff to fetch down toothpaste or shampoo. The only new venture in the town is the mosque, an angular thing of concrete and glass – which, since it is built with funds raised by local Muslims, has taken more than a decade to rise to its present near-completion. There is nothing the town evokes, overall, so much as an open-plan prison, since no space is wasted on pleasure or whim, and no amenities exist save those required to keep inmates docile and alive: the clinic, the sports centre, the fortified police station. If it is unclear what crime Grigny's inhabitants are guilty of, the cynical truth is written up everywhere: in the condescending street paintings of Martin Luther King and Nelson Mandela, and the buildings named after black actors, jazz musicians and sports stars. This is one of France's designated *Zones Urbaines Sensibles* (Sensitive Urban Zones); and everyone knows what kind of bureaucratic euphemism 'sensitive' is.

Grigny has remained famous among the Paris suburbs, but it is no longer for idyllic reasons. It was one of the most violent centres of the suburban riots of 2005, when Grigny youths opened fire on the police and burned down two schools. Just last year, four policemen arriving in Grigny to inspect a vandalised security camera ended up fighting for their lives after a band of hooded teenagers smashed the windows of their cars to toss in Molotov cocktails. State authority is precarious, and the town is tediously accustomed to car burning, gun violence and the drug trade. Recently it hit the international press when it was revealed that Amedy Coulibaly grew up in one of Grigny's housing blocks; a self-declared member of ISIS, the day after the *Charlie Hebdo* attacks in 2015 he went on three separate shooting sprees in Paris, ending up in a siege in a Jewish supermarket in Porte de Vincennes where he was shot dead by the police. But Grigny's notoriety brings about no change and it remains one of the most depressed places in Western Europe: drug-blanched zombies totter in the streets and mothers dream of one thing for their children – getting them out. Impotent local authorities, meanwhile, try to persuade people to reconcile themselves to their lot; the 1970s ziggurats are currently getting a facelift and the town has a cheery new logo.

How did things get like this?

In the 1960s, bureaucrats eyed the small towns to the north and south of Paris with imperial relish, thinking to turn them into warehouses for the capital's working class. Le Corbusier was still the animating spirit of French architecture and planners found in his gigantism a sense of purpose proportionate to their own importance. They commissioned architect intellectuals to build concrete blocks so vast and outlandish that, travelling past them on the suburban trains, one feels closer to Bucharest or Tirana than to Paris. Grigny's blocks, planned in 1967 to house poor Parisians rendered homeless by the redevelopment of the 13th arrondissement, were designed by Émile Aillaud, whose poetic vision of the urban future had won him contracts to re-engineer several French towns after wartime bombs had conveniently removed their centres. Grigny's developments were described as 'utopian', but light, air and modernist sculptures could not disguise the fact that they were, essentially, labour camps. As the old inhabitants drifted away, as the Parisian underclass became distinctly racialised, as the true turbulence stored up in 'scientific housing' became apparent – these camps became ever more determinedly sequestered. Today's mosques – gleaming minarets, paid for, often, with money from Turkey, Algeria or Morocco, are right now springing up all over the suburbs – complete the sense of foreign, middle-income countries nestled in the heart of wealthy France. And given the current intensity of French anxieties about such things, it is not difficult to imagine how stigmatised these territories have become, or how policed their borders.

But as it happens, they are quite effectively quarantined by the Paris-region railway system, which was redesigned when the suburbs were built. The original railway map looked like a fishing net thrown over Paris: the spaces between the main lines were filled in by a dense system of local tracks and one-room stations, so that small towns were as connected to each other as they were to the capital. From the 1960s onwards, these vital capillaries were ripped out. While the lines connecting the capital to its satellite towns were used to forge a new suburban rail system – the *Réseau Express Régional*, or RER – the lines connecting those towns to each other were pulled up or left to grass. The new population dumps had only one purpose, evidently – to supply labour to Paris – and they were not supposed to communicate among themselves. Moreover, since the RER was a stand-alone system, separate from the national rail network, and since its suburban tentacles stretched only so far and then stopped, towns which had formerly been accessible from every direction were now left hanging at the end of a line. No one ever went unless they lived there, and – since visiting a town even five kilometres away could necessitate journeys into Paris and out again – there was a suffocating sense of isolation from everything around.

Where so many people are poor and without private transport, the RER is the only way to come and go – and it has acquired a lugubrious grip over all existence. (Young travellers have mastered a gymnastic substitute to buying tickets: supporting themselves with their hands on the steel barriers, they kick their legs up through the gap between the gates, which activates an emergency sensor on the other side, so the gates slide open.) It is an emblem of exclusion and confinement, as one can tell from the constant references in French rap, whose heartlands are the Parisian suburbs. It is difficult to comprehend how places so close to one of the earth's most significant urban hubs can seem remote until one comes to depend on these maddeningly infrequent trains, which take up to an hour to reach the capital. Then the bleak and denuded landscape makes some sense – and one realises why the jet-setting Parisian elite which runs

French business, politics and culture seems so infuriatingly smug and remote. The car burnings that have become such an emblem of suburban life are very precise, after all, in their symbolism: they are a revolt against the mobile mainstream – against everyone whose rhythms are not drummed out by the deadening stop–start of double-decker trains.

A mere twelve kilometres from Grigny, but a two-hour ordeal on the late-night RER, Arpajon is much diminished from its former self. Even though its population has doubled, there is rather little going on in the town any more: the shoe factory closed in the 1950s and was destroyed in a fire in 1979. The main commercial streets where, in richer towns, there would be clothes stores, bookstores and restaurants, are given over to businesses that produce no bustle: insurance firms, driving schools and, on every corner, real-estate companies – floor space costs not much more here, in fact, than in Bucharest or Tirana, so there is always money to be made.

Looking for morning coffee, I step into a rare open cafe. Like many such businesses around here, this one is run by a Chinese family. Its main commerce seems to not to be coffee or beer but lotteries and horse betting, for which ticket dispensers occupy an entire wall. Several men without drinks – and they are only men – are filling in these tickets, which offer, I suppose, some of the better odds that they will leave this kind of life behind. They are all young, and of North African or Middle Eastern origin. They greet each other with fist bumps and a hand to the heart.

The screen in the cafe is playing a music video by Zayn Malik, the half-Pakistani singer from Bradford, England, propelled to stardom by a TV talent show. The video begins with Malik gazing wearily at the baying paparazzi gathered to catch a shot of him as he emerges from his limousine on a rainy night and disappears into a luxury hotel. Celebrity produces no joy in him. Existence is 'cruel', he sings, as he trudges towards his hotel room. A photographer leaps out behind him, trying to catch another photo, and is summarily dealt with by a bodyguard – but Zayn is too preoccupied to notice, and walks on, hitting his chorus. Life is 'in vain'. He doesn't want to live forever.

Zayn has lost a girlfriend, sung by a ghostly Taylor Swift: this is a break-up song. But it strikes me, not for the first time, how often romantic loss has become just an unfelt convention in pop songs, persisting only as a necessary excuse – or a cover-up – for the real passion, which is not so seemly: that longing for self-annihilation which flows so darkly below the surface of contemporary culture.

I pay for my coffee. '*Merci, monsieur*,' says the Chinese proprietor, '*à la prochaine*.' I leave the cafe and walk up to the RER station where I wait for a while on the platform. I read the posted instructions about what to do in the event of a terrorist attack. Nearby is a flirting pair: white girl and black guy, both in their late teens, both heavily tattooed. The guy starts to kick the girl playfully on her backside. Both are giggling – but he is much bigger than she is and his kicks knock her off balance. She asks him to stop but he is enjoying the game too much. She raises her voice to make herself understood, but then the train approaches and the scene comes to a natural end.

Two hundred and fifty tonnes of red, white and blue train enter the station at 110 kilometres an hour and draw suddenly to a halt. Doors open with a pneumatic sigh and I get in.

We pull out of Arpajon, and I look out the window. Every surface facing the train is covered in graffiti. It is specific to the RER line, for there is not much graffiti in the town. People seem to have walked every last bit of this track, defacing it. We pass a trailer park. The buildings clear and the view opens up onto fields. We draw alongside the pretty River Orge.

I find myself wondering if there is a relationship between the graffiti and the tattoos. Teenagers here are extravagantly inked and they talk about it in a particular way. As a gesture of *reclamation*, as if their bodies were not theirs before. These are people, after all, on whom it has been impressed that their bodies are only lent to them by the state, which will rush to claim them back if they do not treat them as they should. Here as everywhere else, of course, their generation has had to shoulder the burden of escalating paranoia about children's physical safety, and schools are fortified with high steel gates and wide-eyed cameras. But there are added dimensions in the Parisian suburbs: children are frequently taken away, for instance, from parents who threaten their physical security; parents also die young or move away – here, single-parent households represent a quarter of the total – so there are all kinds of occasions to observe how parents are only provisional custodians to a child. Also, in this place where drugs are everywhere, kids are endlessly instructed in the many uses to which they may not put their bodies, on pain of the authorities assuming remote control. The true proprietor of their physical frame is the humourless, preachy state; are tattoos, like the graffiti on the RER tracks, an attempt to deface – and so stake a claim to – public premises? An attempt to spite their own absentee landlords, who have proven so profoundly indifferent to their minds and souls?

In which case, suicide would be a form of destruction of public property.

We arrive in Égly and I get off the train. DANGER! says a sign on the platform. DO NOT STEP ONTO THE TRACKS.

Égly sits on the bank of the river and looks out on the gentle countryside which once made this region so popular. Sitting as it does near the end of the RER line, however, there is a heavy feeling of asphyxiation. Nothing is open as I wander around and there are no people. A dog howls on a balcony where it has been tied up by an absent owner. The street signs speak of decay: the antiques shop, the cemetery, the funeral home, the social centre for the homeless. The regional garbage dump – which seems to be the only motive outsiders ever have for coming here.

There are modest blocks of apartments. Some of the windows allow glimpses of lace curtains of a touching intricacy, harking back to lands far to the east of France; but nearly all have white security shutters drawn down over their windows. The quiet town does not look as though it should be gripped by such anxiety, but everything is barricaded against assault.

I reach the church. Posted outside the door is the list of staff and clergy, who seem to come mostly from francophone Africa. Next to this is the same ubiquitous poster about how to react to a terrorist attack (take shelter behind a solid object, turn off the ringer on your phone). I wander down some narrow lanes. There are ancient, crumbling buildings from the old village days: country dwellings with haylofts and spaces for animals. I pass a shut-up cafe and reach the little police station, which is surrounded by signs saying, MILITARY INSTALLATION: KEEP OUT. Access is through a steel cage. I enter the cage and ring the buzzer: the gate growls and I push on through.

Inside, the nature of local preoccupations is writ large upon the walls. ARE YOU A VICTIM OF CONJUGAL VIOLENCE? Or: STOP JIHADIST RADICALISATION. Or: SEXUAL VIOLENCE: YOU ARE NOT ALONE. Or: JIHADISM: FAMILY AND FRIENDS BE VIGILANT! It is as if the police imagine their entire job to consist of holding the community back from its own will to auto-destruction. If people are not destroying their families, it seems, they are plotting to blow themselves up. The self-culling of a vilified population? To paraphrase La Fouine, the most famous rapper from the Paris suburbs, these towns are cemeteries anyway, even before anyone dies.

A policewoman attends to me, and I say I have a few questions about Égly. She asks me for my papers. I am carrying none. 'This is France,' she shrugs. 'Everything works with papers.'

2

Océane lived in Égly. She had a twenty-hour-a-week contract working in an old people's home.

'I've seen people die,' she said, during one of the online broadcasts she made just before her end. 'Frankly that's not what shocks you. I had a woman who came in and she lasted just two weeks. She arrived and she was fine, she had normal conversations. I have no idea what shit they gave her: the nurses shot her full of medication.

By the end you couldn't understand what she said any more, she was mostly dribbling, even though she'd been perfect when she arrived. I remember she said to me, *I'm going to die, I'm going to die.* So I told her, *Don't worry, everything will be OK, I'm here for you, if you want I'll come and see you in your room.* The next day I turned up at 8 a.m. and she was dead. And what annoyed me the most was they left her the entire day in the room and you had these trainees, these old girls who were like, *Let's go see her, let's go see her!* And I said, *The dead aren't a spectacle for your entertainment.* Then the guy turned up from the morgue and I helped him carry her out.'

Océane was oppressed by the trite and uncaring relations she observed between human beings. She poured scorn on the empty flirtation of social media, the desperate popularity theatre. She had no interest in the artificial animation of alcohol or drugs (though she smoked cigarettes constantly). The dulled existence of the Parisian suburbs, where no one seemed able to engage with anything consequential, depressed her (on the wall behind her as she made her last speech, hung a poster with the words NEW YORK PARIS LONDON HONG KONG). 'I'm half Turkish and half Polish,' she said, in answer to one of the questions posed by her online spectators. 'And no I don't speak Turkish. I don't understand this mania of always asking people's nationality. People are always asking: *How old are you? What's your name? Where do you live? What are your origins?* People are very very very very stupid around here.'

Her relationship with her dispersed family was uneasy, so she did not have the luxury of indifference to this unsatisfying world. *If you were a real Turk your parents wouldn't let you go out with those piercings in your mouth,* said one spectator. 'My father's Turkish,' she replied, 'but I don't speak to him any more. He's an asshole.' Océane's father was a powerful, sensuous individual who took out his moods on the judo floor and the punchbag; his own extensive online life indicates a man prosaically impatient with things intangible or far away. He had daughters from two relationships – the women were not close to each other – but he lived alone and worried frequently about his fading good looks. He ran a popular nightclub just outside Grigny where, in addition to the usual DJ fare, he featured acts like American Borderline, a frat-boy-cheerleader extravaganza including – as his flyer promised – sex toys, strippers, naked teenagers in jacuzzis, strobe showers and many other such marvels, all of it filmed for the American adult media company YouPorn.

In response, perhaps, to such fantasies of youth, eighteen-year-old Océane was committed to an authentic version of her own. She had always found something real in the basic act of care; she had completed a diploma in rescue and safety while still in high school, and perhaps her only moment of genuine élan during the two hours of her broadcasts came when she described her work in the old people's home, which she found '*hyper cool*'. (The bathos of the social media network instantly stole her enthusiasm away again. 'No I don't clean the toilets,' she said. 'I've no idea why you're talking about that.') She kept a cat, too, which found its way now and then into those videos, rubbing itself against her and purring loudly into her microphone. (*You have a big pussy*, writes one wag, as the cat appears in the frame. *Look out we can see your pussy!* chimes another. By this time, her suicide is only ten minutes away and Océane has fallen silent before the dismal stream of commentary.)

She found evident pleasure, also, in taking care of herself – renting a bright studio apartment just two kilometres from where she had grown up in Arpajon. Even on the day of her death, her mass of dark hair was freshly washed, her make-up detailed and immaculate. There were also her tattoos, which she spoke of as a sort of self-care, writing on her body as if she were moving into it – rather as office workers put up photographs and meaningful quotations to personalise an anonymous cubicle.

France is the country which invented for the West the idea of that transcendental romantic love which would ultimately take over every other kind of soul ambition. This French teenager was far from alone in hoping that the spiritual plenitude the world could not give might be recovered in romance, and indeed she had been in a relationship for the past three years. But she felt unloved by her boyfriend and unable to find any echo of her deeper world in him. The situation diminished her. She left him, hoping to take her life back. Shortly after that – as she described in her ultimate video address – she met him again, and he subjected her to violent physical abuse. The thin thread that tied her to the universe had broken. She entered a living death.

'What would make me happy?' she said, in one of her few protracted outbursts. 'Nothing, that's the point. I've got to the stage where nothing can make me happy any more. I can't even find the energy to get out of bed in the morning. You realise that one person can completely poison your life. Our relationship completely destroyed me but he can't understand that because he's a person with no empathy, I mean the suffering of others doesn't touch him. You try and do something to improve the situation, to get people to hear you, but it doesn't work, so . . . With the message I'm going to send out this afternoon I hope he'll finally get it. In this world, unless you shock people, they don't notice, and it has no effect on anything.'

She spoke unsentimentally of her nineteenth birthday, which was to arrive three days after her death: 'I was supposed to do something this weekend for my birthday, I was supposed to go away. But in the end it's not happening, I mean I can't go – because of this thing.' Passing erotic propositions produced wry laughter in her – 'A drink at your place? Forget about it. No actually it's *not* very flattering.'

In the silences, she sighed often, '*Je suis trop blasée.*' The French word has no implication of superiority: it is only empty, numb, indifferent.

The enterprise of 'sending out a message' seems to have given her a renewed sense of energy and purpose. She made a detailed plan and one that was, as events would show, well conceived. She made it known online that she would broadcast some unspecified and sensational event at 4.30 p.m. on 10 May 2016 – using Periscope, a popular social media app which allowed users to stream live video to their followers, who could simultaneously write comments alongside the moving image. She said that she would address her followers in two prior sessions on that same day, also via Periscope, also at prearranged times. Before any of this, she conducted two test sessions to ensure there was nothing she had not thought of.

Suicide then became a technical project, whose organisational demands gave her sudden energy and purpose. She spoke during the sessions about her strategic decisions: 'The advantage of Periscope is that everyone can see it and your broadcast is archived for twenty-four hours.' She gave people detailed instructions about how they could access the feed, and what they could do if they missed it. She kept reiterating her plan: 'Come back at 4 p.m. and I'll tell you all the things I have to say, and you'll see everything that follows. Yes I'll definitely be here at 4 p.m. I can't back out now – you'll see why.' Though people got her talking about lots of different things, Océane was all the time conscious of the job she had to do. 'What time is it? I have three hours left.' *Why can't it happen earlier?* people asked, impatient because nothing much was going on. 'Because there's a schedule. You're all very impatient but you'll find out later on it might have been better not to be.'

'The video I'm going to make,' she said, trying to differentiate herself from social media's general culture of self-promotion, 'isn't designed to *faire le buzz*. It's supposed to make people wake up, to open their minds. I want to communicate a message, and I want it to be passed around, even if it's very shocking.' Her tactic, ironically, was classic social media princess: schedule a big sensation and say nothing about what it will be. But she was hopeful that shock could also produce some return to reality. 'It's the only way to communicate a message. The only way left to ensure the message is taken up . . . Until you provoke people, they don't understand.' (Her French has extra, untranslatable, levels of slangy verve: '*Tant que tu ne tapes pas dans la provoc, les gens ne comprennent pas.*') 'But it's really going to be very, very shocking so honestly I'm telling you that any children watching – and it's got nothing to do with sex – please leave.'

Océane broadcast for fifty-eight minutes in the morning and thirty-seven at lunchtime. For most of that time, she sat on her red couch, speaking into the camera, her face more solemn than overwrought – though she rolled cigarettes and smoked them ceaselessly. At one point she walked out of the house to get her mail from the mailbox (a parcel of make-up, whose contents had been stolen: she showed the eviscerated package to the camera) but otherwise the image did not change. In neither of these sessions did she say what was going to happen, or why; she seemed very much in control of events, and what now looks like apprehension in those videos ('It's so cold in this apartment. I'm so cold') did not seem like it at the time.

At 4 p.m. she came online for her third broadcast. She had said she had something to say, and now she said it. She told people that, a few months before, her ex-boyfriend had raped her and beaten her. Not only this, but he had taken a video of the episode, which he had distributed on Snapchat. Océane gave details of who he was and how he could be contacted. While this was happening, the session started to become chaotic: hundreds of people were joining the feed to see what was going on. Everyone had a point of view: some found her poignant (*The splendour of the world begins with the fragility of a lone woman*), while others took the opportunity to give her spiritual advice (*Convert to Islam and you'll see everything is gonna be great. Allahu akbar!*). Océane fell silent, reading the comments and occasionally rolling her eyes. More than a thousand were now watching and the mood was raucous; people joked about her appearance and expressed lewd anticipation about what she might do, even as others begged them to stop the stream of comments in the hope she might finish what she was saying. Others tried to rouse her from her silence in other ways: *Go on, speak, retard*, or *Show us your tits*, or *I've found my dream, a woman who keeps her mouth shut. Will you marry me?* Someone else proposed a game: *The first one to make her laugh, I'll buy them a Greek* – the promise taken from a rap song by La Fouine, which referred to the *assiette grec* on sale in the Turkish kebab places all over the suburbs.

Océane had retreated behind a persistent smile. The sardonic smile, certainly, of world despair vindicated by dismal evidence. But it also had a dash of real adolescent triumph: *You're going to regret you ever said those things.*

Just before 4.30 p.m., she took her phone, still broadcasting, went out of the house – leaving her cat for the last time – and walked to Égly station, which took just a few seconds. As she got close, the mood among her followers began to change:

> *This girl has no life, why is she coming to tell her life on Periscope?*
> *She's a whore.*
> *She's going to commit suicide, you'll see.*
> *Guys you're really horrible to say such things. She's a human being. Your mother or sister could have gone through what she went through.*
> *Kill yourself.*
> *The idiot's going to harm herself.*
> *Where are you in Égly?*
> *Where is she going?*
> *Stop her, she's going to commit suicide.*
> *Stop that girl.*
> *This is going to finish badly.*
> *This feels bad frankly.*
> *Fuck I think she's going to jump.*
> *Don't jump.*
> *Yes she's scaring me!*
> *Guys can you see the location on her Peri, call the police.*
> *She's in despair this chick she's going to do some bad shit.*
> *Don't kill yourself for a guy.*
> *There's a train fuck.*
> *Fucking hell.*
> *Fuck.*
> *She jumped under a train.*
> *RIP.*

The train hit her at 4.29 p.m., right on schedule. After the event, people remembered hearing her cry out, but that may just have been retrospective fancy. Her phone landed lens down and showed only black, though the microphone was still recording. Was she dead? Was it a hoax? Minutes went by, and they tried to work out the situation from the murmurs in the background.

> *I can hear the firemen.*
> *She's not dead.*
> *I HOPE SHE'S ALIVE.*
> *Oh fuck this is horrible.*
> *Let's pray for her.*
> *She's gone too far.*
> *She gave the number, the address and the FB of her ex.*
> *They're gonna cut the feed now otherwise this is gonna blow up.*
> *It was obvious she was possessed everyone was telling her.*
> *They've found her guys.*
> *Cranial coma.*
> *Show your head dirty whore are you scared?*
> *Cranial trauma.*

At that point the phone was recovered. In the last frame of the feed, a paramedic peered into the screen and pressed the stop button. It was a startling reality effect. But for all those who still believed it was all a hoax, social media users started circulating photographs of the information screens in other RER stations, which announced train delays due to a death on the line.

Periscope has its roots, as Océane did, in Turkey. Travelling to Istanbul in 2013, the two founders had found themselves caught up in the mass demonstrations in Taksim Square, where 100,000 people had gathered to protest against the government's curtailment of social freedoms and the progressive Islamicisation of society. These people were mostly young, and thousands were tweeting from the square; but how much more sensational, thought the Americans, if they could stream live video from their phones. They built Periscope so that people could reveal the injustices they lived with and the world would become a better place. Two years later, Twitter bought Periscope, so rumours went, for $86 million. It is Twitter, therefore, who owns the video files Océane made.

Immediately after her death, the company cut out several key sections from them, leaving only the censored files online. These files were subsequently downloaded by several people and uploaded to YouTube, where they are still readily available. The expurgated sections, however, remain locked up in a Twitter server in California.

3

Thirty seconds before she threw herself off the platform, one of the spectators watching the live broadcast remarked, *Up close, she looks like Nabilla.*

Since the video images of those moments have been wiped, it is impossible now to see what it was in her death mien that would make people think of Nabilla Benattia, France's kittenish reality-TV superstar. But given her stony demeanour over the preceding few hours – the record of which persists – the resemblance seems forced. Indeed, many of the young people congregated for her last addresses found her anything but telegenic. *You're kinda ugly*, they commented. *Your piercings are gross. Dirty whore.* And even – because they were impatient with all the talk and wanted something to happen – *kill yourself. Throw yourself out of the window.*

(As yet, they cannot know how close they aim; indeed she diverts them with false reassurance. 'Don't worry,' she says, still safely installed on her couch, 'I live on the ground floor. What am I going to do? Jump into the street?')

So why, right at the end, did someone glimpse Nabilla in her?

Her broadcasts had gone on for more than two hours by then, during which time people had seen her as she was. Avid for specific detail: *How tall are you? What piercings do you have? Show us your tattoos.* (A heart on her thumb, a red rose on her forearm, which she designed herself. 'The tattoos on my stomach I don't show.') Why did they stop seeing her and see someone else in her place?

In the last seconds, spectators had the sense of something foreign and unnerving rising up in her. *I'm starting to feel her magic inside me*, they said, and it was not quite a joke. *She's going to put a spell on us.* Some alien spirit had begun to emanate from her – and perhaps it was this new presence, rather than the eighteen-year-old herself, that reminded someone of Nabilla. Moments from her death, looking into her phone on the platform of Égly station, she aroused a sudden anxiety in her audience – until then so exquisitely blasé. *Can't you see she's not fucking human? She's a ghost. She's an extraterrestrial. She's a sorceress!*

What was this occult shadow they saw late-blooming in the young woman's face? Was it that curious modern necromancy that had never visited her in life, but which briefly crowned her death, and which – for the very few days her suicide profited the media – she shared with Nabilla Benattia? That high-tech spirit possession we call, for want of a better word, *celebrity*?

For a generation so fully embedded in social media, celebrity was not remote or atypical. It was latent in everyone. Schoolgirls debated with each other how they would deal with its burdens – paparazzi, extreme wealth, film-star boyfriends – when they grew up. And this was not surprising. Social media, after all, supplied a publicity machinery with a reach and power previously available only to truly famous people, and now the condition of the celebrity was everyone's condition. Suddenly *everyone* was broadcasting their life to the world, and measuring their worth on the basis of the libidinal pulses that came back – as only celebrities had before. Suddenly everyone was modifying their human system – their face, their speech, their thoughts – in order that it might interface better with a global technological extension. Suddenly, the celebrity's grief over privacy was everyone's, and everyone was afflicted by her insecurity: *Do people realise there's nothing behind it all except my own frail and disappointing humanity?*

Océane was wired like everyone else. Like many other teenagers, she had often tried to make her image conform to that of the triumphal media funster: there were images of her V-signing in a short skirt and sunglasses on a rooftop in LA, the Hollywood sign glowing in the distance (*You're a real film star*, her friends commented, obligingly). This did not stop her being acutely conscious of – and judgemental about – everybody else's online affectations, but that, of course, was the common paradox. Surveying the great online pageant of self-promotion and superficiality, people were led to believe they were the only ones in the world to have authentic feelings and opinions. 'Fakes' was another English word imported by Océane's French generation, which they used to describe, essentially, everyone other than themselves. *There are only fakes on Facebook. Instagram. Periscope.* But people knew, also, that these platforms had become the custodians of teenage social reality, and there was no question of opting out. Océane was very much in – she had several Twitter accounts, for instance – and even as she railed against what happened on social media, it was on social media that she chose to do it. The only true significance came from mediatisation, and even discontent, if it was to have any meaning, had to be *liked* and *shared.*

The problem was that, for the most part, it did not matter how widely broadcast your discontent was: no one cared. The great majority of celebrities – in this new world where even nobodies were celebrities – were lacking in that basic attribute of the celebrity, which was fame. They were half-creatures – unfamous celebrities, anonymous superstars, VIPs like the entire rest of the world – and unlike their fully formed counterparts, the world did not gasp when they expressed their thoughts and feelings. Everything was lost, in fact, in the infinite cacophony. This was why there was a constant inflation of strategy and contrivance in the social media world;

for even those whose message was *Authenticity!* – those who were sickened by the sensational stunts pulled by everyone else – found themselves inventing such stunts of their own in order for this message to be heard.

Since the events that had happened with her boyfriend, Océane's intimate realm was poisoned. There is no sign that she confided her state of mind to anyone she knew. It was to the broad, anonymous online mass that she decided to unburden herself. But in order for it to mean something, some extraordinary explosion of reality was required. It would have to be of the order of terrorism, which also produced spectacular media effects, and it would probably take her along with it. And so: the macabre theatre of her plan, which transformed her, albeit briefly, into a fully realised celebrity, whose troubled soul was explored in the mainstream news.

Was it this transformation her spectators saw in the last seconds of her life?

There are reasons why the angel of celebrity might float out from her moribund figure in Nabilla's particular guise. Nabilla, after all, was celebrity itself: celebrity in its pure state, uncontaminated by achievement. Five years older than Océane, she had come to prominence on a show called *Reality TV Angels*, where, floating on post-production seraph wings, she revealed herself to be the kind of being that seems designed for one thing: to create electronic waves or, as the French put it, *faire le buzz*. She had a talent for producing deliciously inane aphorisms which so inflamed the network that one had to acknowledge in her a certain kind of contemporary genius. Her legendary catchphrases, from which every other purpose of speech was driven away by the final triumph of narcissism, were shared and quoted and parodied with an almost apocalyptic kind of glee. She seemed made for the end times, in fact – those disoriented times following the death of ideas – for her blithe self-involvement joyfully embraced the emancipation from truth and logic. 'Oh my God,' she said, describing the brutality of a catfight in her reality-TV home, 'it was like the world war of 1978.'

Playing the idiot was a strategy. Nabilla presented herself as pure oblivious physicality, and she proposed that kind of visceral sufficiency that even presidents may depend on today: when everything has become meaningless, there is a reassuring authenticity to bodily impulses, even when they are obscene. And so, when Nabilla's own impulses blew up, causing her to repeatedly stab and nearly kill her fellow reality-TV-star boyfriend, it only inflated her fame (which, as is often the case today, already had contempt as its greater part). Nine days after the suicide in Égly station, and six since journalists had run out of things to say about it, the media turned gratefully to more sustainable fare: Nabilla Benattia condemned to six months in prison for attempted murder. Though, since she had already spent some weeks in preventive detention, she was considered to have already paid her dues and was allowed to go free.

Of course, one did not need journalists to learn this, since Nabilla was delivering it herself, just as she delivered everything else she lived. No Frenchwoman had more Twitter followers than her, who treated absolutely anything as a ruse for self-promotion – including episodes which might have been a source, in ordinary lives, of shame or humiliation – and who was an effortless exponent of coquettish Twitter-ese: 'Announcing something really big soon! Can't say what it is yet! Kisses!' But the channel which really kept her close to her followers was Snapchat, on which she broadcast continually, using its proprietary filters to morph the face atop her bikini-model body into that of an animal: cat, dog or manga bunny.

It was a voodoo-like transformation which carried the frisson of truth. For that condition which Nabilla pursued so savagely, and which we call celebrity, is an irruption of the inhuman into the human. It is the merging of a human core with a far vaster inhuman prosthesis, which then begins to disfigure and consume the original human component – which is why we are constantly seeing the self-destruction of people who apparently have everything; and why suicide, not contentment, is the natural culmination of fame. Perhaps it is for this reason that the Snapchat puppy nose and whiskers deforming Nabilla's face as she walked around in a bath towel gushing about teeth whiteners or shampoo seemed not so much a disguise as an unveiling. Human things had long since been put away from her life. Her impulses were supplied by big data, her tastes were product placement. Her relationship with her boyfriend, which was essential to the marketing fairy tale, carried on: whatever the two felt 'in reality' was suppressed by the relentless electronic reality *show*. Like ancient Egypt's jackal-headed Anubis, Nabilla's dog-headed figure was a visitation from the underworld: it proclaimed the terror of the infernal machine, which offered human beings a new kind of existence, as long as they were willing to have their life energy sucked out in return.

Is it possible, therefore, that there was a more precise kind of revelation behind that remark: *Up close, she looks like Nabilla*? That it was not just celebrity that was seen unfurling in Océane, but that hidden core of celebrity, which is *always about to die*? For, as her infamous outbursts of rage might indicate, Nabilla's reality was not simply the abundance of youth and vitality that her sponsors wanted her to project. Far from it. There was some still-breathing human core even to Nabilla, and this was under assault from the stern, inhuman system which she naively imagined – just as, in a different way, Océane did – she could turn to her own advantage without being consumed herself. 'I'm not doing well,' she wrote to a friend during her trial. 'I've had to give up on certain hopes and I've tried to kill myself . . . Our lives are only passing. I'm weary of it all. I don't know what to do. I'm at the end.'

In the world of social media, where everyone becomes a celebrity, they do not inherit merely the life force of stardom – its beauty, achievement and sex. What is transmitted also to these faceless ranks of superstars is the inner knowledge of death. For, as all true celebrities discover, the media image feeds parasitically on human energy, starving them and removing them, slowly, from the realm of the living. As another animal-headed celebrity once put it – for Michael Jackson too grew a whiskery dog head in his most famous video – a 'mere mortal' is unable to withstand the arcane power of the 'thriller'. His world-domination bargain with the underworld was paid for, of course, with the gradual dissolving of his human form.

Up close, she looks like Nabilla. Days after Océane's death, a number of people who were affected by the story took down their own social media portraits and put up an image of Océane instead. The image was taken from Snapchat and showed her body surmounted with an altered-reality dog head. Her resemblance to Nabilla had become total.

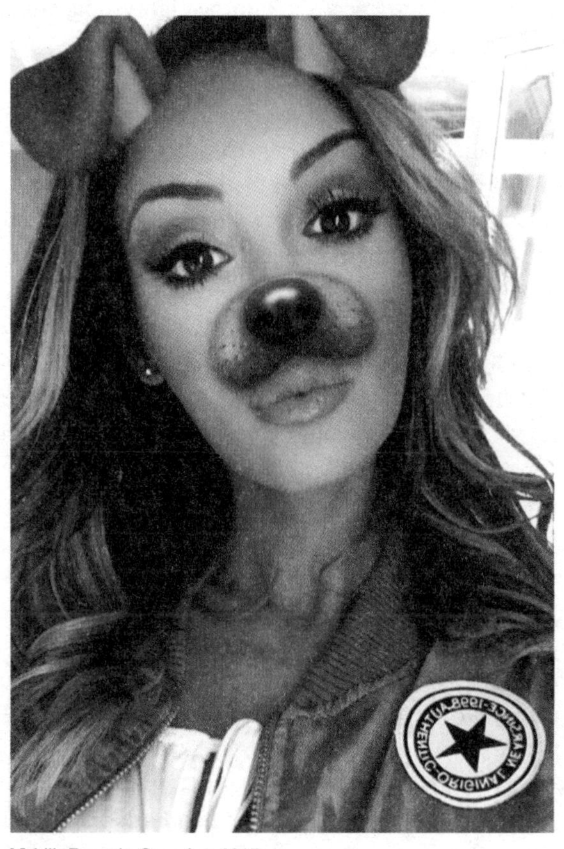

Nabilla Benattia, Snapchat, 2017

4

Ten seconds before Océane threw herself off the platform, someone wrote, *She's strapped herself with explosives, call the police.*

It is not surprising that some people, told to expect a sensational event, expected that. The fatal exploits of Grigny boy Amedy Coulibaly were only eighteen months in the past. It was just six months since the dark night of shootings and suicide bombings that killed 130 people in Paris – including eighty-nine young people attending a rock concert in the Bataclan theatre.

But perhaps there *were* analogies, anyway, between all these happenings. Océane's death was also intended as a kind of detonation, which would 'take out' others apart from herself. On their side, the perpetrators of the Paris attacks were also, let us not forget, bent on their own destruction: they too were suicidal. All these people were young, and nearly all of them had grown up in the racialised ghettos of Paris and Brussels. All of them felt some kind of despair about the reality they lived in Europe, and all of them, crucially, decided that the only significant asset they had, in their negotiation with it, was their own existence.

Though we are familiar with the *statistics* of our monopolistic era, we are far less conversant with its spiritual effects. If mid-twentieth-century Western societies achieved a startling level of consensus, it was due to their extraordinary expansion of the share in the social surplus – to which the destruction (by war) of previous wealth concentrations, and the transformation of 'labour' into 'jobs', were essential. Today, as Western societies reverse those advances and drift back towards nineteenth-century arrangements, it should not be surprising that the malaise, too, is returning from that era. This malaise is felt most keenly by the young, who have seen nothing during their lifetimes save the progressive re-exclusion of the majority from society's wealth, and who embark on adulthood with very little hope that they will be able to 'make it' as their parents and grandparents did. They have a strong sense, in fact, that now-ageing generations have taken everything for themselves, leaving behind only a sterile world – the dwindling species of the earth, the exhausted air and soil – and bequeathing to the young only the burden of their own sins. It is a gruelling inheritance, and one that causes young people, who have the longest futures, to wonder about their endurance.

Malaise takes on particularly acute forms in places like the Parisian suburbs, where work has been informalised and automated almost into nothing: in the most depressed areas, a quarter of young women and nearly half of young men are without jobs. But there too, unemployment is only a symptom of the wider casting out from French society, whose would-be universalism disguises one of the most consolidated systems of power in the Western world. It is no surprise that the pious messages pasted up around these neighbourhoods, which promote the good life of hard work, clean living and happy family – along with the old revolutionary slogan LIBERTÉ–ÉGALITÉ–FRATERNITÉ – are routinely defaced. All that is demonstrated by such platitudes, yet again, is the obliviousness of those in charge, and the inability of the contemporary nation to inspire any kind of allegiance. For many, France has become disgusting, and the impediment to any honourable form of life. As one rap group from Océane's neighbourhood put it, '*Dur de rester halal quand des porcs gouvernent*' ('Hard to stay halal when the country's run by pigs').

This is why the allure of *exit* haunts dispossessed French youth today. The spread of radical Islam is of course one dramatic expression of this: more than 900 young people have left France to go and fight for ISIS in Syria and Iraq, and thousands more have joined jihadist networks at home. But militant Islam is spreading among French youth not just through the radicalisation of existing Muslims, but also through the conversion of non-Muslims who wish to acquire for themselves the activist power it supplies. Those who have turned to Islam in jails, ghettos and gangs represent a significant fraction of France's 200,000 converts to the faith, and a full quarter of those French volunteers to ISIS were also drawn from these same ranks. It was not, in other words, that they were Muslim and therefore wanted to destroy reality and themselves; it was rather that they wanted to destroy reality and themselves – and to rediscover, in the process, some sense of chivalry and nobility – and *therefore* they embraced the trenchant power of radical Islam.

There are many moments in history when young people have dreamed of glamorous self-destruction rather than embarking, drearily, on adulthood. But in all these epochs, those who actually die are the exceptions. Far greater numbers are touched by the same current of despair, but are nevertheless held back from the ultimate act by life's natural defences. These survivors are not left unscathed, however. They live astride the line between life and death, harbouring a kind of sentimental envy for those who have gone. Theirs is a suicide culture, and they lose some of the ability to identify with those who are simply, and unquestioningly, alive.

In the days and weeks after Océane's death, a number of rap 'homages' began to appear online. The rappers were often young men whose unemployment and casual jobs were redeemed by a heroic alter ego: gangster, truth teller and troubadour – even though, in most cases, their 'celebrity' happened in a bedroom, and was known only to themselves. None of them had met the dead girl, but the story of her suicide spoke directly and powerfully to them. Though their rap voices were gruff with urban aggression, the music videos they made were full of starry skies, red roses and slow-motion flapping doves – cut in with the old picture of Océane posing in front of the Hollywood sign – and their words were heartfelt and sentimental. 'My dearest Océane, these verses are dedicated to you / You've gone to be with the angels, what will I do without you?' said one. They wrote about themselves as the tender lovers she never had, and fantasised about having been there to save her. 'I would certainly have been able / To bring you happiness . . . I would have listened to you / So you wouldn't have had to end things.'

But there was something dubious about these offers of help made retrospectively to the living Océane. Perhaps it was because, in general, the singers seemed to have little affection for living people. Even the idea of Océane alive could produce only empty repetition – 'Océane, Océane you were so beautiful / Océane, Océane you were always beautiful' – or lurid banality: 'Little angel who left us too soon / All that will remain is a few photos / A simple life with a childlike smile / A face that ended up covered in blood.' But other living people were spoken of only with hatred and contempt. The greatest opprobrium was directed, of course, at Océane's ex-boyfriend who was a figure of such universal depravity that rappers could speak confidently about 'paedophilia' and 'incest' as well as rape: 'Because of your ex, you went away too soon / He made you suffer incest, my hatred has no words.' But everyone else was implicated too. The people who watched Océane's broadcasts, for instance, were entirely morally corrupt. 'Most of them are whores in fact, and that's the truth,' opined one rapper, demonstrating that Océane's story of male abuse had not persuaded him to alter the way he thought or spoke about women. Women were despicable, just as men were; all were part of the universal corruption. 'People have changed,' wrote one of these same rappers in another song, 'I'm already scared of the future . . . If I'd known human hands were so dirty / I swear I'd have shared my life with an animal.' The living human world was unendingly, incurably degenerate.

Which leads us to the point: that Océane's main merit for these rappers – and the reason why she could be spoken of in such sacred terms – was that she was *dead*. They were not fascinated by the person she had been, nor were they motivated by a general protectiveness towards life. No: they were inspired by the fact that she had made the spectacular decision to leave behind an irredeemable world. In killing herself, she had realised a part of their own fantasy life which they, for their part, could never fulfil – and often they tried to 'borrow' her suicide for themselves, to suggest that they had come very close to that act themselves, and so to include themselves in its glamour: 'I've had those moments / When you feel totally alone / Consumed with torment / I've finished in an armchair.'

Were these just sad loners, expressing extreme, but ultimately anomalous, feelings? Possibly. But it is also the case that they were amateur rappers who copied their styles from more famous figures, and their moods, too, were unoriginal. They were not just expressing their own angst; they were parroting a world despair and a death fascination that was at the heart of contemporary French rap. The world's putrefaction, the unviability of life, the war of the end times: these were the constant themes of rappers from the Paris suburbs, and in several cases the only poetic resolution was that of exit. La Fouine had choreographed his end in a song called '*Quand je partirai*' (When I'm gone) – for how satisfying it was to imagine the world, contrite, at one's graveside: 'The day I die, certain bastards will offer their condolences / Where were they when the unpaid bills arrived?' Orelsan, meanwhile, a white rapper – and France's richest – offered a straight-out suicide note: 'Today will be the last day of my existence / The last day I close my eyes, my last silence. / For a long time I've looked for a solution to these irritations / Now it comes to me, and it's so obvious.'

But if we zoom out from French rap, we realise that teenage culture is touched by the fantasy of exit at a much more universal level. As if to prove, in fact, that such thoughts were not merely their own, many of Océane's obituarists mixed their verses with refrains from well-known pop songs, so endorsing their solitary gloom with the stamp of global celebrity. Several of them borrowed extracts from a hit by the French pop star Caroline Costa (someone else who had become famous from a TV talent show); the song is about someone who is no longer there – for an unstated reason – but once again its power comes from its expression, not of love or longing, but of the emptiness of existence. Hope has become a tomb; happiness is buried; all the petals of life have withered. But if there was one song that showed how far the dream of suicide had risen to compete with romantic love as the dominant feeling in contemporary teenage culture, it was 'If I Die Young' by The Band Perry, a platinum hit six times over in the US which was later featured on the blockbuster high school TV series *Glee*. One of the rappers who recorded a tribute to Océane mixed his words with 'If I Die Young', which was in many ways eerily appropriate to her case, since it spoke of how people only really listen to you after you die. It was a lovely song – a tender love song, in fact, to one's own death – and its particular poignancy is a central one in global youth culture today; the poignancy of the world without me, and the eventual significance and savour of my life when it is viewed by those left behind. How beautiful it would be if I just left. You could lie me down on roses and send me away with a love song.

Océane was the first person to broadcast a live suicide on today's social media platforms. During the hours I spent watching her online videos, however, I never got the feeling that she was, in other respects, unusual. I saw traits in her common to a lot of people these days – and possibly to myself, even if they are most pronounced in the young: she was subdued, serious, intermittently funny, distracted by constant electronic tics, slightly unavailable to herself. She reminded me of a phrase from a recent manifesto written by young French activists, in which they described the condition of contemporary youth: 'expropriated from our own language by education, from our songs by reality-TV contests, from our flesh by mass pornography, from our city by the police, and from our friends by wage labour'. In so many respects, Océane seemed entirely normal, and I sensed that her online exploit, too, would become more customary over time.

During the build-up to her otherwise meticulously executed suicide, she seems to have made one, uncharacteristically careless, omission. In announcing her final broadcast she made it clear that she would block all commentary by followers on the page. She said it several times: 'Later on, when I explain everything to you, I'm going to block comments, which means that I'll talk and you won't be able to write back. And you'll understand why, this afternoon . . . I want you to know that the broadcast I'm going to make, when I'll shut down all the conversations, I want to make it clear in advance that I'm not making it to *faire le buzz*. I'm making it because it's the only way to get my message through.'

But it seems that Océane did not block those conversations, as we have seen. Her last broadcast was engulfed by tides of commentary, and she did not die alone.

How could she make a mistake like that, when everything else was executed with such striking precision? It makes me think of another detail she mentioned in her broadcasts – and one holds on to such details, because she says so little, really, by which one might know her. Recently she had often failed to replace the receiver properly on her intercom, which meant that visitors could not reach her with the buzzer. The postman had to come around and knock on her window – they would chat, and she would not be alone.

Small end-of-life slips.

If Océane was so afflicted by the lack of significance given to human life, it was certainly because she had doubts about her own significance. But that was not the whole of it. She was a sensitive observer, and attuned to the ways in which the scaffolding of human value was collapsing more generally – and, with it, the constraints on people's violation of each other. This was the thrust of her geography, her technology, her generation.

And then, suddenly, she was subjected to the full terror of it: a frenzy of annihilation erupting out of someone she thought she knew well.

After that, she was already pitched into death, and her persisting physical frame was just a kind of after-image. It looked as though she should still possess all the power of the living, but in fact that power was shot through with fatal perforations. The channels of communication between her and the world now opened and shut of their own accord, indifferent to her intent.

Coda

In the months after Océane's death, a Turkish man shot himself on Facebook Live. The next month a pair of Russian teenage lovers live-streamed their last hours on Periscope before shooting themselves dead. Then, in quick succession, three Americans, two of them teenage girls, broadcast their suicides on Facebook. ■

Charles Glass with Ali Qahtan Abdulwahab
Fermajdayi Detention Center, Sulaymaniyah, Kurdistan Regional Governorate, Iraq, 2016

ONE PICTURE, A THOUSAND WORDS

Charles Glass

Fermajdayi Detention Center, Sulaymaniyah, Kurdistan Regional Governorate, Iraq

The young man in the black tracksuit was twenty-one years old. His hair was dark, short-cropped and unwashed; his fingers were dirty but not bruised. There were no torture marks on his emaciated face. He looked dazed as he dragged himself from the cell in which the intelligence branch of the Patriotic Union of Kurdistan (PUK) had held him in solitary confinement for more than a year. He sat on a chair and stared down at the patterned floor. His hands, bound in shiny, chrome handcuffs, rested on his lap. Thus began our interview with Ali Qahtan Abdulwahab – an Iraqi, an Arab, a Sunni Muslim and a former warrior and executioner of the Islamic State.

Ali, the eldest of two boys and five girls by a labourer father, attended school in the hamlet of Ain Saran, near Mosul. The United States armed forces invaded Iraq in March 2003. 'I was eight years old, and I remember it as a dream.' Five years later, a friend from Mosul convinced him to resist the American occupation. 'I joined al-Qaeda.' This began a period of instruction in the use of AK-47 assault rifles and PKC machine guns. In 2010, he was selected for a special assignment. 'We kidnapped a person, a policeman from Hawija.' They spirited the policeman from Hawija, a Sunni town near Kirkuk, to their camp in nearby Tel Eid. His unit's emir, or prince, Mazn Mahmoud Abdulqadir, murdered the policeman with a gunshot to the head for 'training' purposes. The following year, Ali carried out orders to kidnap three more policemen from Hawija. 'I executed one, and the emir killed the other two. Pistol shots to the head. The jihadi mentality was a motivation for me. It never bothered me.'

After most US troops withdrew from Iraq at the end of 2011, Ali said, 'We kept a low profile.' He returned to school and worked part-time in construction. In 2013, al-Qaeda in Iraq (AQI) re-emerged as the Islamic State of Iraq and Syria (ISIS). Eighteen-year-old Ali joined. He did not tell his family. 'In 2014, I pledged allegiance to ISIS leader Abu Bakr al-Baghdadi.' Having conquered most of the Iraq–Syria borderlands and threatening to expand his caliphate to the entire world, al-Baghdadi was at the peak of his ascendancy. ISIS sent Ali south to Baiji, where it was pumping Iraqi oil to finance its operations. He fought against the Shias of the Popular Mobilisation Units or Hashd al-Shaabi. The Islamic State's security department recalled him to Hawija before the Hashd al-Shaabi, along with the Iraqi army, expelled ISIS from Baiji in late 2015. In Hawija, he said, 'We took a training course in how to slaughter and cut heads with a knife. We were a group of eight. They showed us videos.' He worked for ISIS intelligence. 'I was collecting information on people smoking cigarettes, not shaving or wearing the wrong clothes. I reported them. I knew some of them. Three or four were my neighbours. They took them away. I never saw them again.'

While on checkpoint duty: 'I remember that ten peshmerga were captured. They were in the Hawija jail. Later the Wali [governor] of Hawija, Abu Omar, gave the order to a Kurdish mullah, Mullah Shwan, to behead those ten.' Mullah Shwan took him to a camp where ISIS was holding the Kurds. 'Mullah Shwan gave the order to slaughter five of them,' Ali said, in a matter-of-fact monotone. 'I did the job and slaughtered five of them.' The ISIS method was to hold the men face down on the ground, pull back their heads, sever their throats and wrench off their heads. Did they plead for mercy? 'They did not say one word.' I asked what he thought about cutting off the heads of defenceless human beings. Like a death camp functionary testifying at an Allied tribunal after World War II, he answered, 'It was an order, and it was a normal thing for me.'

'Do you have nightmares?'

'No.'

After the beheadings, Ali went back to informing on his neighbours and manning checkpoints, until ISIS found another mission for him. 'An order came in from Emir Ahmed Saleh, a sector leader in Hawija. He sent me and my family to Kirkuk.' Kirkuk, a mixed city of Kurds, Arabs and Turkomans, was by then in Kurdish hands. Ali did not tell his family the reason for the move, thus risking their lives without their knowledge. He shaved his beard to pass as one of many displaced Arab Sunnis unable to live under the rule of the Islamic State and seeking refuge with the Kurds. The emir ordered him to contact eight fellow ISIS undercover agents. 'The plan was to do a vehicle explosion in Kirkuk.' He and his family settled into a camp for displaced people. A month later, PUK intelligence officers arrived at the camp. 'They came specifically for me,' he said. The Kurds took him for interrogation. He supplied them with the names of his eight comrades, all of whom were arrested.

In this dirty war, interrogations are rarely humane. Kurdish intelligence officers confronting a man who had decapitated five of their unarmed comrades would not have been sympathetic. I asked, 'Were you tortured?' For the first time, he looked me in the eye. 'Yes.' How was he tortured? A Kurdish intelligence official interrupted, telling Ali not to answer and me not to ask. That information was 'operational'. I changed the subject. 'Do you have regrets?' Without emotion, he said, 'I feel regret. I have had a lot of time to think. I think they are not on the right path. It's wrong. What they are doing is wrong.' ■

Motion study: male nude, standing jump to right, 1885
Courtesy of the Pennsylvania Academy of the Fine Arts, Philadelphia. Charles Bregler's Thomas Eakins Collection, purchased with the partial support of the Pew Memorial Trust

OUT OF THE CRADLE

John Barth

'I stand here ironing,' declares the narrator of Tillie Olsen's much-anthologized short story of that title. Me, I sit here rocking – in my two-dozen-year-old swivel desk chair at my forty-plus-year-old worktable, between strokes of my Parker (1951 fountain pen) in the seventy-year-old loose-leaf binder (picked up during my freshman orientation at Johns Hopkins in 1947) in which I've first-drafted every apprentice and then professional sentence of my writing life, up to and including this one – my now nearly nine-decades-old body taking idle comfort in the so-familiar oscillation that has, this workday morning, caught the attention of its octogenarian mind.

Nothing vigorous, this rocking: just a gentle, intermittent back-and-forthing as I scan my notes and exfoliate them into these sentences and paragraphs. Notes, e.g., on the ubiquitous popularity of rocking chairs (including the iconic John F. Kennedy Rocker), porch swings, hammocks and the like: a popularity surely owing to our body's memory of having been calmed and soothed through babyhood in parental arms, cradles, infant slings – a bit later on rocking horses. And in adulthood, a particularly delicious feeling for my wife and myself was the gentle rocking of our cruising sailboat at anchor in one of the many snug coves of Chesapeake Bay. These calmative effects no doubt derive from our prenatal rocking in the womb as our mothers went about their pregnant daily business, themselves rocking in chairs now and then to rest between stand-up chores and to lull their increasingly active cargo. We are not surprised to hear from neuroscientists and physicians that rocking releases endorphins, which abet our physical and mental health – though one also remembers the furious, feverish rocking of the never-to-be-soothed protagonist in D.H. Lawrence's ironically titled 'The Rocking-Horse Winner'.

Old-timers, especially, favor rockers as they circle toward second childhood, and nursing homes, particularly ones for patients with dementia, are more and more using rocking chairs as therapy: thus from 'Rock-a-Bye Baby' we rock and roll our way to Hoagy Carmichael's 'Rockin' Chair'.

'Out of the cradle endlessly rocking,' writes Walt Whitman of the waves of Long Island Sound, 'I . . . A reminiscence sing.' A boyhood beach memory, it is, of his having sharply pitied the keenings of a male mockingbird bereft of its mate: desolated love-cries that the Good Gray Poet is pleased in retrospect to imagine having inspired his whole ensuing poetical life's work. And that he now 'fuses' with the sea's 'low and delicious word' – 'death, death, death, death,' – to arrive at an intellectual acceptance and emotional transcendence of The End. Not for us to question whether, in Whitman's case, the poem's conclusion declares a psychological accomplishment on its author's part or merely raises a hopeful/wishful possibility.

In my own case, as befits a mere novelist, the out-of-the-cradle-rocking reminiscence is more prosaic: for the first seventeen-and-then-some years of my life – from babyhood until college – it was my fixed nightly habit to rock myself to sleep. Left-side down in bed, I would roll gently back and forth into oblivion at a rate slightly lower (so I've just confirmed by comparing kinesthetic memory, surprisingly strong, with my watch's sweep second hand) than my once-per-second normal pulse. About 1.5 seconds per rock it was, by my present reckoning, or forty rocks per minute – which I now further discover to approximate my most natural-feeling frequency for desk- and rocking-chair rocking as well. Try it yourself, reader: once per second feels frenetic, no? And once every *second* second a bit laggard? When 'restive' (odd adjective, that; it sounds as if it ought to mean rest-*conducive* rather than rest-*resistant*), I would rock even in partial sleep.

I learned of my rocking habit from my twin sister, whom it never seemed to bother in the ten or so prepubescent years when we shared a bedroom (with, appropriately, twin beds); perhaps she was inured to it from our months together in the womb. And so I was reminded further and less patiently by my older brother in the several subsequent years of our room-sharing, between my puberty and his departure for college and military service, through which interval I troubled his repose with my rockrockrocking and he mine in turn, more intriguingly (if I ceased rocking and feigned sleep), with the soft slapslap of adolescent masturbation, which his kid brother was only just discovering. And so I was reminded finally by the teasing of college roommates, who pretended to think I must be jerking off in some exotic wise when, too ashamed at that age and stage to rock myself to sleep, I sometimes embarrassed myself and entertained them by rocking *in* my sleep.

An old-time Freudian, one supposes, would maintain that it was in fact masturbative, that rhythmic back-and-forthing that wore away the shoulder of my teenage pajamas from friction against the bed-sheets. But hey: masturbation as far back as pre-kindergarten? Sure, our hypothetical Freudian would reply: all toddlers play with their privates until shamed out of doing so, whereupon the instinctual itch finds other outlets, or inlets. Yes, well, maybe: but about my rocking as a mode of post-pubescent-though-still-virginal Getting It Off, I feel the way Robert Frost felt about his critics' reading his 'Stopping by Woods on a Snowy Evening' as a poem about the death wish. When I write a poem about death, Frost maintained in effect, I write a poem about death. When I want to write about stopping by woods on a snowy evening, I write about that. Or, more directly to the point, the young woman in one of Bruno Bettelheim's classes whose knitting during his lectures reputedly so distracted the eminent psychiatrist that he admonished her publicly by declaring that what she was doing was a sublimated form of masturbation – to which she spiritedly replied, 'No sir, when I knit, I knit. When I masturbate, I masturbate.' By age fourteen, when I was inclined to whack off I whacked off. Rocking myself to sleep was a different business altogether.

Which is not to deny any twenty-first-century holdout's contention that even to the busily copulative and/or explicitly masturbatory, the gratification of rocking in bed – yea, even of rocking in a desk chair or front-porch rocker – may have a mild erotic component. If so, however, then like reflexology or floating on gentle sea waves (in my experience of giving or indulging those pleasures, at least), it's more assuaging than arousing to the carnal itch – rather like 'shuckling', the Jewish custom of swaying back and forth while reciting the Torah. Anyhow, as a wise philosophy-professor used to remind us Hopkins undergrads, one arrives at generality only by ignoring enough particularity: the more a proposition applies to everything in general, the less it applies to anything in particular. If my real subject were erotic gratification, I'd be 'off my rocker' to write about rocking myself into the arms of Morpheus in bedtime years of yore and into fruitful intercourse with the muse in desk-chair work-mornings since.

Right?

Not quite right, in this context. That old slang expression for 'crazy' – which my *Pocket Dictionary of American Slang* dates to circa 1930 (the year of my and my sister's birth) but gives no derivation of, as does neither my *American Heritage Dictionary* nor my compact *Oxford English Dictionary*, sounds turn-of-last-century mechanical to me, more in the vein of 'slipped one's trolley' than of a senseless 'out of one's chair'.

In any event, my infantile habit disappeared, rather swiftly and painlessly as I recall, during that freshman college year, thus sparing me the embarrassment that I used to fear more than my roommates' teasing: that I might unconsciously fall to rocking while sleeping with a woman when that eagerly anticipated time arrived, and frighten the bejesus out of her. And there've been no relapses in the decades since, although even nowadays my wife will sometimes ask me please to quit distracting her by rocking in my chair when we're reading or TV-watching in a room together. Recliners I can do without, but if there's a rocker I'll go for it; and only with some effort eschew its intended function.

Meanwhile, back on campus, this then-new loose-leaf binder was filling up with lecture notes and term-paper drafts, its divider tabs labeled EUR HIST, LIT CLASSICS, POL SCI and the like, instead of their present WIP [work in progress] #1 WIP#2, etc. – the former for front-burner fiction in the works, the latter for essays, lectures and such miscellanies as this. By sophomore year I had managed to get myself duly and rockinglessly laid and had amended those notebook-dividers, replacing JOURN[alism], my tentative original major, with something like FICT 101. The exact name of the university's introductory fiction-writing course escapes me (Hopkins's brand-new degree-granting creative-writing program was one of only two such in the nation back then; nowadays, for better or worse, there are above four hundred), but not the trial-and-error pleasures of fumbling my way into Vocation.

In those green semesters of literary (and, coincidentally, sexual) apprenticeship, did I have a swivel rocking chair? Not impossibly, although it and the desk it served will have been among the battered Goodwill Industries cheapos wherewith we all furnished our off-campus student-warren, row-house walk-ups. What strikes me now – what nudges my patient Parker 51, anyhow – is that it will have been just about when I ceased rocking myself to sleep that I awoke to my calling and commenced my curriculum vitae as a desk-chair-rocking Writer (and, coincidentally, lover/husband/father). What had formerly been a sedative, a tranquilizing soporific, had morphed into a facilitator of reflection, contemplation, deliberation, even inspiration: in both aspects, one supposes, a channeler and discharger of mild but maybe mildly distracting nervous energy.

So? Sixty years on, a veteran wordsmith now but still a novice octogenarian, I find my musings sometimes preoccupied with that latter datum and, by obvious extension, with my mortality: a preoccupation that, while often sharpening the pleasures of a many-blessinged life, sometimes dulls their edge and threatens to preempt my professional imagination. Unlike Walt Whitman, I do not find the sea's 'low' word 'delicious' and reconciliatory, much less inspiring; I find it quietly chilling. Death (and worse, one's own and one's mate's approaching infirmity, dependency, bereavement, and the rest) *inspiring*? One would have to be . . . *off one's rocker* to find it so! Or else believe in some Happy Hereafter – which I utterly cannot.

How then to come to terms with The End, except – small comfort, but doubtless better than none – by fashioning sentences, paragraphs, pages out of its inexorable approach, while not for a moment imagining that such wordsmithery will delay by even 1.5 seconds the thing's arrival?

I rock and consider, in pensive (though not in wordless) vain . . . ■

'State of mind' is defined in Merriam-Webster as a person's emotion or mood, in other words, as a kind of internal human weather, turbulent or calm, sunny or gloomy, hot or cold. That climate is sometimes clearly visible on a person's face or in her posture, but not always. (Inner states can be hidden.) And like the shifting patterns of actual weather, states of mind are unstable. In a moment, one mood may become another. I cannot remember what I was thinking when my sister called to tell me our father had died, but the thought, whatever it was, fled my mind and was instantly replaced by the work of absorbing the truth of his death. The phone call changed my state of mind in seconds. I am often amazed at how dramatically sunshine lifts my mood and how quickly clouds depress it, how listening to Bach's cantata 147, 'Jesus bleibet', inevitably sends me into a rapture of tender, high feeling, no matter how glum I may have been before the first note sounds. There are poems by Emily Dickinson I read to induce a state of mind: a radical, vivid, fierce clarity I find nowhere else: 'He stuns you by degrees, / prepares your brittle substance / for the ethereal blow'.

Often before I fall asleep, I enter a state of loose reverie. My eyes are closed, and my thoughts variously jolt or dance or lapse fluidly from one associative thought to another, and my mood seems to chase the words or pictures that rise unbidden to mind and either ease me into slumber or prick me awake. It is not simple to draw a hard line between states of mind and our perceptions of the world, our memories of it, or our imaginative fantasies that draw from both perceiving and remembering it. The world as we experience it is in us and of us. My father is no one now, not a person anymore, and yet he has haunted my dreams for thirteen years, and dreams are most definitely states of mind, another form of consciousness and another form of perception, not of the outside world directly but of its residue reconfigured in the hallucinatory phantasms that visit us nightly.

When I was very young, I believed my mother could read my state of mind. When she doubted my honesty, she would say, 'May I look into your eyes?' If I was innocent, I would gaze soberly into those maternal eyes. If I was guilty, I would squirm and resist the test. My mother obviously did not need to be a clairvoyant to gauge my truthfulness. All she had to do was look at me. But long after I had given up thinking of my mother as a supernatural being, I found it unbearable to look her directly in the eyes and tell an untruth. She was, I think, my conscience incarnate. My guilt was bound up with her gaze. Infants are not guilty. Like shame and pride, guilt is a social emotion born of our attachments to others, and that form of self-punishment only becomes active once a person is able to see himself as others see him. It is born of reflective self-consciousness. My child self could not bear to be seen as a bad person by my mother because as she looked at me I saw my sorry self through her eyes.

It is a cultural habit in the West to think of the mind as a locked room, a sealed adult domain that thinks, calculates, and makes decisions, wise or unwise, but which is fundamentally isolated from the minds of others. Many hundreds of thousands of words have been written about the problem of other minds. How do I know you are not a zombie, someone who walks and talks and acts a lot like me, but has no consciousness? And if you are human, your internal weather, your sunny days and gusting winds, your high or low temperatures are not mine, and unless your face is a map of your moods or you tell me about them, I will not know what is happening in your mind. And then, even if you do tell me, you might be lying and lying far better than the four-year-old Siri lied.

I expect every person has been deceived, lied to and betrayed.

We misread others and suffer for it. We also often read the minds of other people with a high degree of accuracy. And we don't just witness the moods of others; sometimes we catch them. Emotions are contagious. A toddler hurts himself, falls down and the unhurt child watching him begins to howl. Feelings spread as yawns do. We do not plan to come down with another person's mood, but it steals inside us anyway. Empathy is a shared state of mind, one feeling in two persons or three. Your sadness becomes mine. My empathy may become a vehicle of insight for me and therefore help me to help you or it may debilitate me altogether, make me so sad I am no good to you whatsoever. Empathetic states are not necessarily beneficial to either person, but the fact that these states exist is further testimony to the truth that human beings are social animals – we rely on other animals like ourselves to become ourselves.

I have been living with the same person for thirty-six years. I cannot read this man's mind. He has anterooms in his personality I strongly suspect I have never seen. Mysteries abound. And yet time has produced an uncanny mental mirroring between us. A friend tells a story, and it triggers an immediate, identical association in each of us. Before my husband opens his mouth, I know what he will say or before I speak, he knows what I will say. The link between the heard story and our spontaneous double response is rarely obvious and why our two heads have summoned the same material at the same instant strikes us as inexplicable. It happens again and again and more and more. It may be that two minds with years of talk and grumbling and fighting and laughing and all-around bumping into each other behind them have states of mind in common. The winds rise, and the clouds begin to move, and the sun comes out at just the same time in two heads rather than one. ■

Danez Smith

crown

i don't know how, but surely, & then again
the boy, who is not a boy, & i, who is barely
me by now, meld into a wicked, if not lovely
beast, black lacquered in black, darker
star, sky away from the sky, he begs, or
is it i beg him to beg, for me to open,
which i do, which i didn't need to be asked
but the script matters, audition & rehearse
the body – a theatre on the edge of town
chitlin' circuit opera house, he runs a hand,
praise the hand, over me, still red with hot
sauce, is that what it is? his hands, jeweled
in, what? what could it be? what did he pull
from me? a robin? a wagon? our red child?

//

pulled from me: a robin, a wagon, our red child
with dead red bird in his hands, dead child
in red coffin on wheels, parade out of me
second line up the needle & into the vial
all the children i'll never have, dead in me
widow father, sac fat with mourning, dusk
is the color of my blood, blood & milk
colored, chalk virus, the boy writes on me
& erases, the boy claps me between
his hands & i break apart like glitter
like coke, was there coke that night?
my nose went white then red all over
thin red river flowing down my face
my blood jumped to ask him to wade.

//

my blood got jumped, ask him to wait
before he gives me the test results, give
me a moment of not knowing, sweet
piece of ignorance, i want to go back
to the question, sweet if of yesterday
bridge back to maybe, lord bring me
my old blood's name, take away
the crown of red fruit sprouting
& rotting & sprouting & rotting.
in me: a garden of his brown mouth
his clean teeth, his clean answer
phantom hiding behind a red curtain
& i would sing if not for blood in my throat
if my blood was not a moat.

DANEZ SMITH

//

if my blood was not a moat, i'd have a son
but i kingdom myself, watch the castle turn
to exquisite mush. look at how easy bones
turn to grits how the body becomes effigy.
would have a daughter but i am only
the mother of my leaving. i sit on jungle gym
crying over other people's children, black
flowers blooming where my tears fall.
bees commune at their lips, then
turn them to stone. as expected.
my blood a river named medusa. every man
i touch turns into a monument. i put
flowers at their feet, their terrible stone feet.
they grow wings, stone wings, & crumble.

//

they grow wings, stoned wings, crumble
& fall right out my body, my little darlings.
i walk & leave a trail of my little never-
no-mores. my little angels, their little feathers
clogging the drain, little cherubs drowning
right in my body, little prayers bubbling
at the mouth, little blue skinned joys
little dead jokes, little brown eyed can'ts
my nursery of nunca, family portrait
full of grinning ghost, they look just like me
proud papa of pity, forever uncle, father
figure figured out of legacy, doomed daddy.
look at my children, skipping toward the hill
& over the hill: a cliff, a fire, an awful mouth.

//

& over the hill: a cliff, a fire, the awful mouth
of an awful river, a junkyard, a church made
from burnt churches – place for prayer
for those who have forgotten how to pray.
i stand by the river, the awful one, dunk
my head in the water & scream
for my river-bottom heirs – this is prayer
right? i fall & i drown & i trash & i burn
& i dunk my head in the water & i
call the children drowned in my blood
to come home – this is the right prayer?
lord, give me a sign, red & octagonal.
god bless the child that's got his own.
god bless the father who will have none.

//

god bless the father who will have none
to call him father, god bless the lonely
god who will create nothing. but there's
pills for that. but the pills cost too much.
& the womb cost money to rent.
but who will let you fill them with seed
from a tree of black snakes? but i didn't know
what he was bringing to me. but he
told me he was negative. but he wasn't
aware of the red witch spinning
in his blood. but he tasted so sweet.
sweet as a child's smile. sweet as a dream
filled with children who look just like you
you know: black, chubby, beaming, dying.

//

you know: black, chubby, beaming, dying
of hunger, dying on the news, dying to forget
the news, he came to me like that. we were
almost brothers, almost blood, then we were.
good god, we made a kind of family – in my veins
my son-brothers sleep, sister-daughters
name each cell royal, home, untouchable.
in every dream, i un- my children:
untuck them into bed, unkiss their lil wounds
unteach them how to pray, unwake in the night
to watch their little chests rise & fall, unname
them, tuck them back into their mothers
& i wake up in bed with him – his red, dead, gift
i don't know how, but surely, & then again.

SALVAGE

Reynaldo Rivera

Introduction by Chris Kraus

Twice this week, I go to my friend Reynaldo Rivera's house to look at his photographs. He lives in a big Victorian mansion next to a body shop in LA's Lincoln Park that he bought seventeen years ago.

Reynaldo tells me: *The earliest memories I had of feeling something was suffering. That feeling you have when someone leaves you.*

Throughout the 1980s and 90s, Reynaldo photographed his world, a world that no longer exists in LA, of cheap rent, house parties, underground fashion and bands and three Latino gay/transvestite bars: Mugi's, the Silverlake Lounge and La Plaza. In LA's Latino subculture then, gay male and transvestite bars were the same thing.

Except for La Plaza, these bars are long closed and most of the performers are dead. But in Rivera's astonishing body of work, these men and women live on in a silvery landscape of makeshift glamour, the only true kind, a fabulous flight from unacceptable reality. Their glamour was salvaged from old, late-night movies from cinema's golden age in Hollywood and Mexico City. Tiny, petite Salvadorean Gabby wears a rabbit-skin bolero over a ruched, sequined tutu; her hair styled in a perfect Louise Brooks brunette bob. On another night at La Plaza, she poses backstage in a long-sleeved white leotard and garlands of ninety-nine-cent store holly and pearls around her wrists and her neck. Olga, wearing a short, teased blonde wig and drop earrings, props up his angular chin with his hairy and muscular arm. Yoshi, the Japanese owner of Mugi's, wears an enormous toque hat, a feminized version of Hugo Ball's Magical Bishop, over a low-cut beaded gown. In subsequent photos, she has a scar from a knife fight slashed across her left cheek.

Most of the photos were taken backstage, *where it all happens*, as Rivera knew. Half in and half out of costume, Olga, a short-haired, middle-aged Mexican man with thick glasses, grins and offers his arm to a tall girl in full Vegas regalia teetering on a pair of spike heels, as she looks down into her G-string.

When he was fourteen and working at his dad's liquor store in Mexicali, Rivera watched his father shoot a prominent gangster over a minor dispute about whether the store carried a particular brand of beer in a forty-ounce size. The gangster stumbled out to the street, where he died. His dad fled with his son's green card, leaving Rivera to cross the border alone. From Calexico, Rivera went back to his mom's house in LA, and then up to Stockton, where he and his father picked up seasonal work in a cannery and shared a hotel room. It was there that he found his first camera in a pile of fenced goods. He stole books of the works of Lisette Model, Henri Cartier-Bresson and Brassaï from a local thrift store, bought dozens of rolls of 35 mm film, and learned the rest on his own. His first photographs were of the mother and daughter who cleaned their hotel.

I thought if I could capture these moments, he told me, *keep them on file, I could find some kind of order. It was everything to me. I started capturing, documenting, for lack of a better word, the things that I saw. It was a kind of alchemy.*

These are provisional notes. Looking at Rivera's photographs, I remember LA as it was when I arrived in the 90s. Meanwhile, the old wood-frame houses in his once-immigrant neighborhood are being sold, bought, painted and fenced and then flipped like a long stack of dominos. Soon, I will write more. ■

Colin Grant and medical student friends on the eve of their college ball, 1981
Courtesy of the author

THE RECALL OF HERMAN HARCOURT

Colin Grant

Mile End Road, coming to an abrupt stop at the intersection of Cambridge Heath and Whitechapel, is so called because it's exactly a mile from the City of London. I know this because Herman Harcourt told me so. But then in the same breath, he also said that he'd more than once walked the entire length of Mile End Road heel-to-toe and that it had seasonal variations, contracting seven feet in the winter. For weeks he'd been alarmed about the shortening, worried that maybe his feet were still growing, before arrving at this welcome revelation. Herman considered himself something of an amateur anthropologist of the East End, but he wasn't always a reliable witness on account of his condition.

A not-so-contestable fact is that in London's rush hour you'll find at least one schizophrenic on every double-decker bus – that is statistically 1:100. This was one of the first things we learned in medical school in 1981. This, along with our tutor's mantra that there was pathology all around us, and that we should pay close attention. 'Think pathology; always be thinking pathology!' But how do you get from pathos to pathology? And once you arrive, is there any way back? Although I didn't frame the question like that at the time, a version of it haunted me throughout my first year as I made my way along the Mile End Road to Whitechapel each day, either on foot,

Undergound, bus or bicycle, from my shared house in Bow. There was plenty of pathology on view – TB, bronchitis, tertiary syphilis and myriad mental illnesses. Of all the schizophrenics who joined the number 25 bus on that short stretch during rush hour, Herman Harcourt was the most frequent.

The first time I came across Herman there was something familiar about him. Exiting from Whitechapel station, I heard a loud and distinctive speaky-spokey, West Indian voice. As we squeezed past the ticket collector's box and spilled out onto the pavement, above the sing-song tirade of stallholders, discounting fruit and veg, offering 'Pound o' bananas fifty. Pound o' bananas fifty', you could just make out that singularly Caribbean accent in the distance, shouting what sounded like 'Knee grows occurs'.

His words were high-pitched; the man appeared to be hyperventilating. The gaps between his shrieks shortened until they merged into a prolonged awful-sounding howl. At the same time, all along the pavement, one cluster after another, the pedestrians began to part. Someone or something was coming and could not be stopped. People peeled away as if instructed. It all seemed bizarre; as surreally choreographed as those feathered showgirls on television in the black-and-white musicals I'd sat through on Saturday evenings, raising their plumes in sequence to reveal, finally, the tap-dancing stars in dinner jacket and sequined evening dress.

This particular Fred Astaire turned out to be Herman Harcourt. He thrust through the mass of people on that sweltering afternoon, wrapped in a heavy overcoat with a piece of cord pulled tightly around his waist and emerged just as I knew he would, in line with the onset of déjà vu, that elusive and uncanny feeling of events unfolding marginally ahead of your memory of them.

He was no more than fifty, but old enough to have been my father, and was obviously on the run, perhaps from a shopkeeper. In each hand he gripped numerous bulging plastic bags; they formed a ring around him as encumbering as any Victorian lady's layer of petticoats and his voice became increasingly strident and urgent until what he was actually screaming became clear: 'Negroes are cursed!'

This strange bagman was bearing down on me and I could move neither left nor right, backwards or forwards. I was gripped by a paralysis and a collision seemed inevitable. But somehow, with his plastic bags flapping at his side, Herman brushed past, so close there could not have been a piece of tissue paper between us; so close I caught a whiff of the fug of sweat and tobacco on his dirty overcoat.

He easily outpaced his pursuers, a man and woman in their forties. If he'd continued, he might have got away, but he suddenly stopped and began walking backwards, retracing his steps precisely and nervously, as if in a minefield. When he reached me, he put down his bags, bent over and picked up a cigarette butt, pinched it back into shape and shoved it into his coat pocket. That's when they caught up and pounced. Not in a rough way; more like anxious parents who had lost their child in the crowd. I've often wondered why Herman stopped. It seemed such an odd thing to do. Everything might have turned out differently had he kept on going.

'Don't let them take me,' Herman pleaded. 'Please! They're impostors. Don't let them take me!'

By now the man had put Herman Harcourt in an armlock. 'Do not be alarmed, he is harmless really,' he said. 'No need for alarm, is there Herman?'

'Ah who you a-call Herman?'

'I am just saying that you are harmless, are you not? I am paying you a compliment, Herman.'

'Listen how the man call my name. Is so you call me name, in the street? In the street?!'

'Now Herman,' pleaded the man.

'I know you?'

'Hermaaaan, pleeaasse.'

In the absence of anyone else foolish enough to slow down and pay attention to what was going on, Herman turned and confided to me: 'Me nah know the man, you know.'

He scrutinised his captor, searching for clues, until he found that which confirmed his suspicions.

'Look at his feet. Him an impostor. Didn't I tell you? Him an impostor, man. Just look at his feet. You see any sock on the man feet?'

Though the man wore sensible black patent-leather shoes, Herman Harcourt was agitated and exercised over his absence of socks. I confess that I too thought it curious.

'But Herman, you are not wearing socks either,' said the man.

The news hit Herman hard. He trembled. Seconds passed, perhaps a minute before he steadied himself and was brave enough to look down. 'Oh Lord dem gone with me socks!'

Herman's anguish was pitiful, but the man seemed amused by the direction the conversation had taken. His laughing lips were held in check only by the vexed gaze of his colleague, who had a professional tenderness about her and a countenance more in keeping with a chaperone.

The setback with the socks was enough to remind Herman – how could he have forgotten? – that 'Negroes are cursed!' He repeated this endlessly, as if gamely trying a tongue-twister. 'Negroes are cursed! Negroes are cursed!' He broke free from the man's grip. He turned and turned, not moving from the spot, like a child trying to make himself dizzy. Finally, he slumped. He couldn't raise his suddenly heavy head; his chin rested on his chest.

The minders propped him up like cornermen to a boxer at the end of a bruising round. After some adjustment of positions (the choreography appeared to have been thought through), all three were ready to move off, not quite arm in arm but linked to such a degree that if one moved the others were bound to follow. Before they reached the corner, Herman turned back towards me. Would they allow him a word of advice to the young man? He didn't wait for permission, but shuffled in my direction. His chaperones, loosening but not releasing their grip, snaked along with him.

'In private, a word in private, if you please,' he whispered.

The woman straightened the collar of Herman's overcoat and smoothed the lapel with the back of her hand. 'No more secrets.

Remember? Who said that? Did you say it and not mean it? Was that you being insincere?'

Herman shook his head vigorously.

'Good. So what is it you want to say?'

'All I wanted to say to the young man . . .' Herman began graciously, but almost immediately his tone hardened. 'Because he looks like a decent young man, although looks can be deceiving. I wanted him to know, looking all smug and pleased with himself . . .' He paused to jab a finger at me. 'Brutus. Et tu, Brutus! I come not to praise him. He knows what he's done. But I want to offer a word of advice, my friend. If they come for me in the morning, they'll be coming for you in the afternoon.'

The chaperone squirmed as she tried to fashion some kind of apology. I thought to lessen her discomfort by saying to Herman that I had no idea what he was talking about. Except I'd met men such as Herman Harcourt throughout my young life. Yes, we Negroes were cursed, but I'd been schooled to break the spell; to confound expectations by exchanging the factory floor (which had been the lot of my parents) for medical school. That was the assumption that had been deeply invested in me. Perhaps it had once been invested in Herman too, but he had defaulted to that older, more persistent preconception of our limitations. If Negroes were cursed then men such as Herman were carriers of, and became, the virus. If he was the virus, I was the vaccine. The bagman's presence though – his very being – mocked the notion that my contemporaries and I could escape the accursed path predetermined for the black man.

Herman's eyes blazed with passionate intensity as he continued, with a note of compunction in his voice, 'They'll be coming for you in the afternoon. If not today, then tomorrow.'

'We are the Ocean, you are the sea,' chanted a group of lads as they joined the number 25 bus at Stepney. The Ocean, the name of their gang, referred to the Ocean Estate, which was made famous by the local R&B singer Leslie Charles, a Trinidadian immigrant who tipped his hat to the place he grew up by taking as his performing name: Billy Ocean.

'We are the Ocean, you are the sea, sea, sea,' they continued to chant. They were loud but harmless mostly, though I recognised one or two who were a menace to cyclists. It was always a risk to ride along Mile End Road as the schools got out. Kids from the Ocean would wait at the bus stop to shower any 'middle-class bike-riding wanker' with gobs of spit as they passed by.

Thankfully they didn't recognise me off the bike. My medical-student eyes were in a steady state of readiness, on the lookout for individual forms of pathology. I clocked a schizophrenic as soon as he got on at the next stop. Black and older than average, he shuffled along like a child in his father's slippers. He stepped through the doors in the middle of an intense conversation, although he had no companion. A new idea seemed to come to him with every breath. I had the feeling that he was trying urgently to exhale unpleasant thoughts. He breathed in, he breathed out. He breathed in . . . He started to flounder. His arms flapped. He spun around. 'Please, somebody. Help. I can't . . . I can't breathe.'

No help arrived, but eventually the hyperventilation subsided. It was difficult to 'read' what was going on. The man's face was obscured by sunglasses and a huge floppy cap (the type worn by Rastas) though he seemed to have little hair. Trapped food had dried on the beginnings of a beard.

People moved back into their seats, further than was necessary, drawing their coats more tightly around them as he moved down the aisle. The pall of lost ambition, suggested by his clumsy oversized jacket and stiff, stained trousers in need of a wash, was communicated even more fiercely in the assembly of plastic bags containing the detritus of life – books, rags, clothing and sandwiches that were turning green – that he gripped in each hand. He was followed down the aisle by a small-boned builder, his face cracked and speckled with plaster. The builder stared disapprovingly as the schizophrenic took occupancy of a pair of seats.

'Not too clever, is it, mate?'

It'd been a long day and he'd had to put up with enough shit already, thank you, and he was minded to exert his native right to a seat in his own fucking country. He pushed aside the schizophrenic's bags. He didn't care if the brown brother stank worse than rancid Gorgonzola or that there were fossilised woodlice in his turn-ups. He was going to take his birthright, what his grandfather fought Hitler for: a seat, mate, all the fucking way to Aldgate.

The schizophrenic moved out of the seat to make room for him. Through the sunglasses his searching eyes caught mine and before I could look away he had worked his way to the seat beside me. In a sea of miserable faces, my determinedly neutral expression must have seemed comforting, not to mention my colour. It was only then that I recognised him, yet he seemed unaware of who I was.

'Countryman, how far this bus reach?' he asked.

It was hard to believe that this was the same man I'd met the week before; astonishing that he could have deteriorated so much and so fast. Everything about him repelled, but more than that I was acutely aware of his colour – black like me, and wished he wasn't. For a moment I contemplated speaking French and feigning ignorance of English, but faltered at the end.

'Where are you heading?' I whispered.

'Port of Spain. That's Trinidad,' he added.

'Are you kidding?' I smiled.

'It look like I joke to you? It seem say it a joke?'

There was no mistaking his seriousness. 'No, no,' I answered. 'You look deadly earnest.'

'But wait!' He pulled up smartly and said, ever so slowly, 'Ernest my middle name.'

'I'm sure it is, Herman.'

'What the rass! How you know my name?'

It was then that I decided that I couldn't stay in the conversation any longer. I stood up, inched past him and pulled the string cord overhead to signal to the driver that I needed to get off at the next stop.

'We are the Ocean, you are the sea!' The gang renewed their chant.

The chanting caught Herman's attention. He looked up from smoothing his plastic bags.

'Noooo,' he smiled. 'It's "that was the river, this is the sea", isn't it?'

The gang stopped their chant. One of the members peeled away and moved down the aisle, pointing towards Herman. 'Cunt!' he said, and the others took the cue for this new chant. 'Cunt! Cunt! Cunt!'

The bus pulled up at the next stop and I disembarked at Stepney Green without giving enough thought to what might happen next. Some of the gang were black, so Herman should have been all right. But for about five minutes I didn't turn round, not for fear that Herman had followed me, but out of worry that he hadn't; that he was still on the bus with the Ocean.

'Before we start,' said the patient. 'Just one t'ing. I not gwan have your finger up me arse.'

The doctor looked up from his desk, closing one unwieldy bundle of notes and opening another. 'Ah, good morning, Mr Harcourt.'

'Promise!' said Herman. He was sickly, thin, with a scruffier beard than when we'd last met. I was less sure of how old he might be as he was one of those men whose body had resisted middle age and was only now beginning to turn. His brown skin was younger than his years; smooth except for a line of suspicion that marked the brow of a hyper-expressive face, fit for a mime artist. 'Say it, say it or write it down,' barked Herman. 'I will not poke me finger up Mr Harcourt arse.'

'Oh, I shouldn't think that'll be necessary,' the doctor assured.

'Why not?'

'Now Herman . . .' Dr Gordon half turned to me. There was the faintest suggestion of a raised eyebrow. He flicked through his notes attempting, but not quite managing, to disguise his boredom. There was a forced quality to the action; more, I felt, for the appearance of thoroughness than the expectation of some sudden insight.

'So Mr Harcourt, what can I do for you today?'

Mr Harcourt's mind was elsewhere. He had only just noticed me, and he looked alarmed.

'This is . . . What was your name again?' asked Dr Gordon.

'Grant,' I said.

'Grant, that's right. This is Grant from the medical school. He'll been sitting in on the surgery for a few days.'

'A junior doctor?'

'Yes, a medical student. A first-year medical student, actually. Rather unusual. Don't ordinarily let them loose on the public so early. We're privileged. Young Grant here must be something special.'

I had become accustomed to the admiration of black people whenever they heard of my beautiful career and I was quite skilled at adjusting my expression to evince the appropriate degree of racial pride and humility. But Herman looked incredulous, even hostile. Nothing in his eyes suggested that he recognised me. He lifted his chin and spoke in a jumble of words that appeared to be from a made-up African language or an approximation of one. Dr Gordon just about managed to suppress a smile, and encouraged his patient to sit down. After a while, keeping the full beam of his eyes fixed on me, Herman reached out, gripped the edge of the chair and worked his way into the seat.

'Have you check him paper qualification?' Herman asked, cupping his mouth with his hand, before whispering to Dr Gordon, 'You know what them like. Could-a pick it up at Brixton Market.'

I waited for Dr Gordon to intercede, but he merely smiled the way a dog owner might do when their pet jumps up at you. There was also the possibility that he felt it was an argument between two black people and that he was disqualified from intervening.

My doubts about Dr Gordon had surfaced that morning, starting with the red Porsche parked outside. This was not Knightsbridge; this was Bromley-by-Bow. He might have been forgiven the signet ring worn on the little finger of his right hand and the manicured fingernails, but the Porsche seemed a vulgar display of wealth in such a poor area.

I should have stood up for myself, but in the midst of arranging the sentences in my head, Herman was given a plastic pot and asked to produce a sample of urine, and instead of retiring to the toilets he simply pulled out his penis and filled the pot. Even after nearly six months at medical school, that fell outside the spectrum of what we had come to expect. And yet again Dr Gordon reacted as if it were no more unexpected than a dog cocking his leg at a tree.

I did little to disguise my abhorrence. I like to think it signalled one of those moments of forfeiture when the brother 'tek the shame'. But I couldn't really be sure that anything had passed between us because Herman only had eyes for Dr Gordon. It was apparent that he'd been in and around hospitals over the years. He laid before the doctor a catalogue of ailments in just such a manner as I had seen and heard senior registrars do when summarising a patient's condition to the consultant on a ward round. Using language that was both precise and highfalutin, he spoke with the relish of a man who has been starved of intellectual company.

My scalp began to itch. I had the peculiar sensation that Herman, though speaking to the GP, was actually addressing me; that there were hidden messages that would be undetected by Dr Gordon; that it was a form of code black people adopted when white people were present.

I hadn't heard Herman articulate a specific complaint other than that he wasn't feeling right. 'Something is wrong' was as far as he was able, or prepared, to venture when asked, and yet the GP was already scribbling on a prescription form and ticking boxes on it.

'Working?'

Herman didn't answer.

'When was the last time you worked?'

'I haven't worked for the past . . .' Herman broke off and then continued, 'I'm not working for the past, I'm working towards the future.'

Dr Gordon laughed, thought about it again and laughed some more. He tore the prescription note from the pad in a single unbroken movement that brought to mind someone peeling a plaster from a healed cut. He held out the note for Herman and, for the first time all morning, the doctor smiled with conviction. 'Don't let the buggers grind you down.'

Herman still wouldn't look my way as he prepared to leave and I, equally, couldn't bring myself to look at him. But just before he reached the door, he turned and mumbled some more Africanesque at me; then he was gone.

'Quite the scholar, our Herman,' said Dr Gordon, clicking the top back on his fountain pen after finishing up the notes. I had thought so too, in the way he'd used a battery of words – 'distempered', 'dyspeptic', 'ennui' and 'egress' – that were then unfamiliar to me.

'Yes, he certainly has a big vocabulary,' I agreed.

'No, I mean literally. A linguist, I think. Hence the Kiswahili. He has a PhD.'

'A PhD?' I immediately regretted the incredulity in my voice.

'Unless he bought it at Brixton Market. Ha ha ha! But no, Dr Herman Harcourt used to be a university lecturer. Pitiful really.'

I could hear a stream of Kiswahili now on the other side of the wall, but not consistently so. The Kiswahili morphed into Jamaican patois and then back again. What had puzzled me before about Herman's accent was how it ranged around the Caribbean islands. It wasn't specific. What Dr Gordon said now made sense. There was a performative quality to Herman's speech; a kind of playful ventriloquism. But whether it was Kiswahili, Jamaican or Trinidadian, there was no mistaking the bite of argument and irritation in his haranguing conversation with the receptionist next door. The receptionist wanted him to move on; he was reluctant to leave. When Dr Gordon asked me to find out what was going on, I had a sense that Herman was playing for time and actually waiting for me.

In truth, I'd have liked to have gone to him and drawn up a couple of chairs so that we could sit and talk softly. I'd have apologised for abandoning him to his fate on the number 25 bus the week before; I'd have confessed that when I observed him closely I had the queer feeling of looking into a mirror of the projected future, of perhaps seeing how easily his fall could be a rehearsal for my own. I said none of these things.

The traffic was backed up to the east all along the road just past Brick Lane, close to Aldgate East Undergound station. Motorists leaned out of driver-side windows, craning their necks to try to see what the hell was going on. Three police cars approached the Tube station, surrounding a bus which appeared to have broken down; more police cars were arriving – with their sirens blaring – inching their way past the stationary traffic. The passengers spilled out from the bus onto the pavement. The driver stepped out too and, bizarrely, seconds later the doors closed behind him and the bus lurched forward.

I struggled to get through the mass of people blocking the entrance to the station. Such was the density that for more minutes than I was comfortable with I couldn't move at all. Without my prompting, one of the passengers said, 'Some loon trying to get to Trinidad or somewhere. I dunno. Daft bugger's gone and hijacked the bus.'

But the hijacking was cut short that instant when half a dozen policemen stormed the bus. Seconds later a couple of officers got off the 25 with a wild-eyed black man who was armlocked between them. An ironic cheer went up from the people on the pavement. I pressed on through the melee, determined not to look back towards the bus, and eventually broke free from the crowd into the atrium of the Tube station. As I descended the steps into the bowels of the station, I heard the hijacker cry out, 'I know that man! I know that man!'

Built originally as a workhouse in the nineteenth century, St Clement's Psychiatric Hospital had a twelve-foot-high perimeter wall and a heavy wrought-iron gate as a further safeguard against escape.

I had been assigned to 'special', that is to look after just one patient; to act almost as a 'professional friend or chaperone'. The patient had been sectioned months before (the term of his legally binding involuntary incarceration had expired), but he'd since developed anxiety about leaving the grounds of the hospital, even about leaving the ward. I was unsurprised to learn the name of the patient. It had begun to seem as if some irresistible outside force was pulling us together.

Herman Harcourt slept soundly in a high bed, covered from head to toe in a single white sheet, shrouded like a mummy. I sat beside the bed and waited for him to wake. A ward porter, a fellow Caribbean kinsman, looked in on the room and, seeing my black face, sidled up to me and burped through Guinness breath, 'Poor man drug up to him eyeball.'

In our previous encounters, Herman had appeared to be continually on the move. Sleep, even if enforced through medication, must surely have come as a release from that febrile state.

An hour passed and I could not resist the temptation to gently pull back the top of the sheet to confirm that it was indeed Herman. Even as he slept I glimpsed, as I had on that first occasion at Whitechapel almost a year before, the air of a man in exile or retreat from himself, and one who was not yet fully cognisant of the fact. After another hour he began to stir.

'I didn't think you were ever going to wake up,' I said.

Herman yawned, shedding the residue of sleep. 'Man nah dead; coffin nah sell.' His eyes swept round the room. Saliva had been pouring from the edges of his mouth. I reached into a pocket, pulled out a handkerchief and handed it to him.

'You're giving me this?' He began to cry. Tears of appreciation streamed down his cheeks. 'You're really giving this to me?'

The door to the dormitory was half ajar and he asked me to close it. When I returned to his bedside, he was beaming.

'Man I knew you'd come.'

'You knew?'

'How did you get in?' he whispered. 'What's the plan?'

I told him that he was confused; that I probably wasn't who he thought I was.

'Of course,' said Herman. 'I get it.' He put his index finger to his lips. 'Shhhhh, we mustn't let on. You're a stranger to me.'

'I am a stranger to you.'

'Yes man, me understood. So what's the plan? You give a sign or signal? I wait for the signal?'

After a while I managed (and this would be the case in subsequent weeks in Herman's company) to turn the argument. I suggested we go for a walk where he could clear his thoughts; it was to be the first of many, designed progressively to wean him back into society, to overcome his agoraphobia. On day one we walked out of the grounds down Mile End Road for a hundred yards and then returned to St Clement's. On day two we doubled the distance, and on day three we trebled it.

At first I was, I confess, embarrassed to walk with him, especially after being instructed by the ward sister to link arms in case he was suddenly overcome by an urge to run off. In many of the shops Herman's reputation for soliciting credit and reneging on payment preceded him. Whenever we approached a grocer's, tobacconist's or off-licence, Herman agitated to switch sides so that he could be closer to the road and buffered by me if he was spotted by one of the irate and unforgiving shopkeepers.

In walking with Herman along Mile End Road it was possible to gauge the stages of his pathology through the landscape. From Grove Road west to Cambridge Heath, I logged the scholarship boy's ruined ambition: the Underground station where his voice gave out when he was desperately trying to busk; the crossroads by the oval synagogue where he caused a massive blockade by standing in the middle of the street to direct the traffic; the Radio Rentals store where he had begged for the first time from a startled young black man who placed a coin in his hand.

My initial reluctance to be associated with Herman stemmed from his lamentable condition. It served as a reminder of my own frailties and the pressure I felt to stick to and stay on the course at medical school, even as evidence came daily that I was unsuited to it; to reward my family's considerable investments (emotional and financial) in me. The yearning to flee from that responsibility was near constant. Herman had clearly escaped his own familial expectations by taking flight into madness.

With time I found myself looking forward to our promenades and peculiar conversations, often punctuated by lucid intervals when Herman cast me as the son he never had, a son who might learn from his wisdom and mistakes. And slowly my outlook began to shift from 'thinking pathology' to considering the pathos of Herman's predicament – though he would have rounded on me ('Save your tears for the deserving,' he'd say) if ever I nudged the conversation towards any expression of pity or compassion.

One late afternoon, spying an acquaintance in the distance whom he was keen to avoid, we took a detour from our normal route and ended up on a back street in Stepney Green where Herman had a council flat. He still had a key and persuaded me to make a pit stop to gather a few possessions. We had to force ourselves in past piles of unwashed clothes and half-eaten plates of furry and crusted food. I could only speculate about the unhygienic awfulness of the toilet because Herman was adamant that it was out of order. Then, having gathered a bundle of shirts and trousers from the flat, and despite my protestations that we were already late for returning to St Clement's, Herman refused to leave. When I asked him when he would be ready, he answered, 'Never.'

Here was the moment I had always feared when accompanying Herman – a shearing away from our shared reality and a turn towards an interim state that might lead to a florid psychosis. That 'never' seemed to come from somewhere and someone else. Almost in the same breath Herman beckoned me over to the bed to help him lift the mattress. Underneath were a slew of dirty magazines. That was to be expected, but in between the copies of *Men Only* and *Penthouse* were clumps of ten- and twenty-pound notes. As I lifted the mattress, Herman swept them all into a plastic bag. There must have been several thousand pounds.

I should have jumped in and said something, anything. In my stupefaction, Herman laid out the most ridiculous plan, fuelled by a mania that suggested his mood-regulating medication was wearing off. He could not return to the hospital. To go back was to confine himself to loss, to no life; he would never be considered sane again. The only sensible course of action would be to take the money and fly back to Antigua (wasn't that just brilliant?) from where he had arrived thirty-five years before. It made perfect sense, didn't it? And I could go back with him; yes, we'd be fellow travellers. In any event, we could discuss the details en route, on the bus, the Underground and the plane. We had to get to Heathrow fast before his/our absence was detected – because we were in this together now and there was no going back. None whatsoever. There was no time to lose.

Herman was out the front door before I could process any of what he was saying. I followed lamely in a daze as he made his way to the Underground, first onto the District Line and then changing to the Circle. We spoke non-stop; but I was aware that I argued unconvincingly because some part of me was attracted to the folly, to the roll of the dice, to jacking it all in and not answering to anyone.

Round and round we went on the Circle Line, perhaps three times before the realisation, like a cold snap in the pit of the stomach, began to sink in that all this talk was madness.

'Is this it?' Herman asked every few stops. I shook my head and brushed away the tears that were in danger of coming. Somehow, after yet another circumnavigation of the Circle Line and then back onto the District Line, I managed to convince Herman that we'd arrived at the stop for Heathrow and not in fact at Mile End. 'Quick time, quick time,' I encouraged Herman as we hurried off the carriage and out of the Underground. It was only when we emerged onto the street that Herman understood my treachery. 'Negroes are cursed!' he screamed. 'Negroes are cursed!' He fled before I could lock arms with him.

He moved with surprising speed, shuffling along quickly with short steps. Just a few hundred yards away, though, he pulled up abruptly. He seemed unconvinced. Having made too good a job of his escape, he now looked worried that he'd not be caught. Amid the roar of traffic, Herman hesitated. He'd have been swept up into the air by the wind if there was any; he could go neither forwards nor backwards. He froze in front of a street lamp. It was dusk and the lamplight began to fail, to give out – on, off, on, off . . . He tried to work out the sequence of the code. He counted the beats between each glink. But no matter how hard Herman willed the sequence to continue, the lapse between each surge of light grew longer until the street lamp finally, stubbornly, refused to restart, its message left incomplete.

I caught up with him and led him towards the hospital. He recoiled, pulling against me ('Merciful Lord, help!'), but really he put up limited resistance and quickly gave in to the inevitable, surrendered as he knew he must, as he so often had, to the greater will, to the allure of someone with a clearer sense of the way ahead. ■

The English side, before the injuries.
Eastern Mediterranean University Stadium, Writers' World Cup 2016, Cyprus
Courtesy of the author

CYPRUS UNITED

Joe Dunthorne

It was the opening ceremony of the Writers' World Cup 2016, hosted by the Turkish Republic of Northern Cyprus, a country that does not exist. Five local dignitaries sat in wooden chairs on the running track, their suit jackets glowing metallic in the sunshine. We, the athlete-writers of England, with our recurrent back problems, our knee supports, jogged onto the pitch for a photo call. Along the far touchline there were fifty students from the local university, each one carrying a different national flag. In actual fact, there were just eight teams in the competition, and two of them were Germany. The Germans had brought one team to contain all their wheezy middle-aged novelists, and another team to actually win. We resented them for this because we had not thought to do the same. 'Eye of the Tiger' blared through speaker stacks as we stood reddening in the sunshine, waiting to play our part in history.

The big event at this Writers' World Cup was the prospect of the first semi-official game in over fifty years between teams from the north and south of Cyprus. With the island torn between the Turkish-occupied north and the Greek Cypriot south, and UN peacekeepers patrolling the buffer zone between them, arranging competitive football matches has not been high on the political agenda. But football is still a useful way to view the country's situation. The

Turkish Republic of Northern Cyprus is, under international law, an illegal occupation of the island, and so their football team is barred from all official competition. They are in the unfortunate situation of being lectured on ethics by FIFA. This means the Northern Cyprus football team is forced to play matches only against other unrecognised states. There are regular tournaments precisely for this purpose, featuring such fixtures as Heligoland vs Chagos Islands, or Occitania vs Abkhazia. The Turkish Republic of Northern Cyprus is the current world champion of countries which don't exist, after beating Zanzibar on penalties in the final.

By contrast, the Greek Cypriot team – which is to say the official, FIFA-endorsed national team of Cyprus – are welcome to play football on the world stage. Their problem is that they almost never win. In their entire history, they have not qualified for a single international tournament. It's easy to see how the two teams might benefit each other, one offering visibility, the other talent. Of course, it's not that simple.

This is where writers' football comes in. In its ideal form, the embarrassingly low skill levels of the writers' game, combined with the empathic powers of literature, create an atmosphere of productive humility in which to broach sensitive issues. And with guaranteed crowds of fewer than fifteen, the stakes could not be lower.

So we stood on the pitch beneath Mediterranean skies, watching for the arrival of the Greek Cypriot team. We'd heard that their match against the team representing Northern Cyprus was due to take place in the middle of the island on a neutral pitch inside the 180-kilometre-long buffer zone that divides the country in two. But as 'Eye of the Tiger' continued to play – the lyrics encouraging us to enjoy crushing our rivals – there was no sign of the Greek Cypriots. Nobody could say exactly what had happened. Were they just skipping the opening ceremony or boycotting the whole tournament? And if they were boycotting the whole tournament, did that mean the tournament was not as humble as we'd believed?

Before the first game kicked off, we were each given welcome packs. They contained a self-propelling pencil, a prospectus for the Eastern Mediterranean University who were organising the tournament, and a T-shirt that showed a man kicking a football so hard that it broke free of its chains. The slogan underneath said: FOOTBALL WITHOUT BORDERS.

We lost our first match against Austria but remained good-natured. We congratulated them after the game and agreed we would later swap shirts, though ours were expensive replica England shirts and theirs were just plasticky red knock-offs, sponsored by a hydroelectric energy company. We were the very embodiment of goodwill.

Our second match was against Germany. We learned that the reason the Germans all looked tanned, rather than sunburned, was because they had arrived two days early, 'to acclimatise'. It is an embarrassing cliché to say that we quickly developed a special resentment for the Germans, but football – even writers' football – is a friend of the embarrassing cliché.

The referee blew his whistle. 'We can do this, England,' I found myself yelling, despite my Welshness, despite my half-German mother. I was not the only player transformed by regressive instincts. Our captain, Andrew Keatley – a soft-voiced writer of brilliant, searing plays about injustice and humanity, about guilt and inheritance, an outspoken voice for the voiceless – spent the ninety minutes shouting at the Germans, shouting at the referees and linesmen, and generally sending the message that their voices were irrelevant. I had never really given much thought to the fact that Andrew had no hair until I saw him screaming in an England shirt. He was suddenly Plato's eternal skinhead: the ideal form of the worst in our culture. Even our critically acclaimed poet, Nathan Hamilton, headed the ball with such commitment you could almost smell the poems evaporating. It became clear we all badly wanted to destroy Germany. We wanted to do it for England. I recalled the incident when the writing hand of Marcus du Sautoy, The Simonyi Professor for the

Public Understanding of Science and Professor of Mathematics at the University of Oxford, had been ruthlessly crushed, bones and all, in collision with a German writer of plays for children. I vowed to avenge his months of lost productivity. The idea that football might provide an opportunity to overcome our dumber instincts seemed ridiculous now: football was a chance to set our idiocy free.

We won three-nil. We beat Germany three-nil. In the World Cup. We tonked them. We mullered them. We shellacked them. All the made-up words. We did not care that the only audience for our victory was a handful of Cypriot weightlifters, dead-lifting dumbbells at the side of the pitch. We refused to acknowledge that the Germany B team was any worse than Germany A.

'Germany's Germany,' we said.

Back at the hotel, we drank, swam, watched traditional local dancing, and told stories of our heroism, our darting runs and crisply pinged through-balls. We mythologised our best goal, how the ball had seemed to hang a moment in the sky – spinning on its axis like the earth itself – before novelist Matt Greene – never forget his name – had slammed it home, bringing to a righteous end one of the great feuds in world history.

I have since rewatched a video of this game. It is amazing how slowly we move. It looks like we're on the moon. In order to make the game on the screen accurately reflect my self-image, I played it at three times real speed.

The next morning, we woke up as our old selves again. We got the news that the Greek Cypriots were definitely boycotting the tournament. As we padded around our five-star all-inclusive hotel in free slippers, we began to understand. Even when football claims to mean nothing, it means something. We realised then that the only Greek Cypriot presence at the tournament was one of the England team. Our team contained Canadians, Scots, Germans, Danes and, on this occasion, Jimmy Roussounis, a British-born Greek Cypriot, who lived in the south of the island. He was also our unofficial tour guide. He gave us some insight into why the Greek Cypriots might not have turned up. Our hotel, for instance – the Salamis Bay Conti – had been owned by a partnership of Greek Cypriots and Brits when the Turkish army invaded in 1974. Now it was run by Turkish Cypriots. This meant that, according to international law, each time we dived into the sparkling waters it was a further act of trespass and illegal exploitation. Jimmy didn't feel very happy staying there. He said he was taking small comfort in the thought that he was sleeping in a British-owned room.

There was also an unsettling sense of how much money had been spent by the Eastern Mediterranean University, which is a Turkish Cypriot state institution, in order to allow a hundred mid-list foreign writers to have a weekend eating baba ganoush in the name of international football. We enjoyed a swimming pool, a private beach, Thai massage in the wellness spa, an almost-permanent buffet and grill. It was wristband paradise. For the first time ever, we were being treated like actual footballers and there could be no justification for this that had anything to do with football.

That afternoon, Jimmy took us south from our hotel to Varosha, the ghost town, a huge area of beachfront hotels and apartment blocks, formerly the tourist hub of Cyprus, now rotting and decrepit. In 1974, years of tension between the Greek and Turkish communities finally exploded. The Greek nationalists staged a coup, ousted the president and started a period of military rule. In response, the Turkish army invaded. When the army entered Varosha, the 39,000 people living there fled the city, leaving their businesses and homes behind them. They never returned. The area is now cordoned off by the Turkish army, rows of high-rise buildings rusting photogenically in the glow of the turquoise waters. When we visited, a Turkish soldier – one of 30,000 still posted on the island – was standing on a rooftop, keeping guard, his main purpose to stop tourists trying to take photographs. We could just about see the old Argo Hotel, where Elizabeth Taylor and Richard Burton used to stay. The side of one building had fallen away to reveal an elevator hanging on its chain like an avant-garde chandelier.

At the far end of the beach, we saw an old couple sunbathing on deckchairs, reading the newspaper, chatting idly as though they weren't sitting in front of rolls of barbed wire, a sign with a picture of an armed guard and the words FORBIDDEN ZONE in six languages. This couple were probably old enough to remember when the fences weren't there. The beach still looked beautiful, as long as you didn't glance behind you.

Amidst all this, we bravely continued to play football. We took on Austria again, winning this time, and got hammered by Northern Cyprus. They had an ex-semi-professional on their team who took an impressive free kick, simultaneously scoring a goal and injuring our goalkeeper, who tore his rotator cuff while failing to stop the ball.

By the Sunday afternoon, the main factor in the success of each team was the number of injuries. Lumbars were strained, ankles turned, hamstrings pulled tight. The changing rooms reeked of Deep Heat. Fifty per cent of our older players were 'carrying a knock'. For the penultimate match, the organisers arranged a friendly – The World vs The World – with all the players who could still run assembled into two teams. It was like a Benetton advert without the grace or beauty. I scored a header, assisted by a pinpoint cross from a young German performance poet. I forgave all previous grievances.

The winners of the Writers' World Cup were the Hungarians, though there was general agreement that they had cheated, not through actual cheating, but with their youthfulness and skill. Were they real writers? How could they be? We all agreed that talent on the page was inversely proportionate to talent on the pitch, so these players were surely not published. At dinner that evening, one of the Germans went from table to table, asking each of the Hungarians to recite a poem from memory to prove themselves. We googled the publishing history of the boy who'd scored the winner.

On the final day, we attended a panel discussion on the theme of Football Without Borders. The talk was hosted by a former Turkish football commentator whose muscles rippled beneath his polo shirt.

A view over the fence into Varosha, the ghost town.

There was some pleasure in watching the translator listen attentively as he talked incessantly and without pause, building clause upon clause, forever finding new energy, even as everyone in the room willed him to stop. Days passed. Eventually he paused and looked to the translator. She said: 'He welcomes you all and makes a joke – but that is behind us now. We move on.' Whether this display of putting bad times behind her and moving on was intended as a satire on the peace process, we never got the chance to ask. The event was running long and so, halfway through, she had to leave for another appointment.

A few months after we returned to the UK, we saw in the news a photo of Ban Ki-moon holding the hands of leaders from both Turkish Cypriot and Greek Cypriot communities and saying that a solution was 'very close'. It seemed that, where writers' football had failed, the UN might succeed. But within weeks, the talks had stalled. President Erdoğan – in the run-up to the Turkish referendum on his new powers – had decided to take a strong position on Cyprus. He said Turkish troops would not withdraw unless Greek troops did the same.

This summer, the Turkish Republic of Northern Cyprus will host the CONIFA European Cup for states, minorities, stateless peoples and regions unaffiliated with FIFA. And no, CONIFA is not a joke name. It stands for the Confederation of Independent Football Associations. Their tagline: freedom to play football. Northern Cyprus will be joined by Abkhazia, South Ossetia, the County of Nice, Karpatalya, Ellan Vannin (aka the Isle of Man), Székely Land and Padania. The website shows a photo of a glamorous hotel with jetties that pitch out into the turquoise waters. They wisely do not provide the hotel's name or address so I am unable to check its ownership status. It looks newly built but it may just be refurbished.

At the time of writing, the Cyprus national team are in good shape to fail to qualify for another European Championship. They beat Israel but lost to Bosnia–Herzegovina, Belgium and Greece. You'd think the Greek team might have taken pity on them. But there's no room for empathy in the beautiful game. ■

Students parade the flags of countries not in attendance.

Supple, wily Monster of mine;
You wait for one of those mornings when I wake up thinking ill of myself in a fretful, petty way. I've been in too many discussions about the pros and cons of Botox and facelifts. Yesterday a young woman at the gym told me how terrific I looked, then added *I wouldn't think you were more than* ______ and threw out a number higher than I would have wished.

I go to the kitchen. I can't find the mug I want. I go to the bathroom. The container with my sterilized cotton balls is stuck. I'm furious: what did Carmen do when she came to clean yesterday – did she break the mug and not tell me? How did she close the container so tightly I may have to take a screwdriver to it?

I'm seized by a thought.

If I were a white slave mistress this is the moment I'd call her into my presence, rail, slap her, throw an object – maybe the container – at her and warn her she'd be whipped if it happened again.

If I were a high-handed white woman in New York City, I'd chastise her sharply the next time she came here. If I were angry enough maybe I'd fire her.

If I were a high-handed woman of color – black, brown or beige – I would do the same thing. And decide to hire a white cleaning woman so I could feel less guilty about my tone.

I get the container open with no screwdriver and no damage to my nails. It had probably tightened when Carmen polished it. I find the mug – I'd left it in the dishwasher – on the shelf where it belongs, with other mugs.

If I'd called Carmen and spoken sharply to her, would I apologize?

On the phone or in person? If I apologized would she stay on? I know she needs the work. How would we proceed? Would we perform our old cordialities or adapt slightly: she more distant or more anxiously obliging; I more distant or more strenuously gracious.

Monster says: We're done with that. Let's move on. Today's a day for you to feel blocked and impeded; a coward in work and love; resenting duty; suspecting pleasure. It's time to blame your parents, and to do so properly you must be artful and nuanced. You must be literary.

Monster sends me to a quote from the wise and balanced Willa Cather.

'Even in harmonious families there is this double life . . . secret and passionate and intense . . . Always in her mind, each member is escaping, running away, trying to break the net which circumstance and her own affections have woven around her . . .'

Of course I need my own variations, I know that.

'Daddy, daddy, you bastard, I'm through.'

Sylvia Plath is overused, says Monster.

'My dead mother gets between me and life.'

Romaine Brooks. Not bad but too general, says Monster.

My parents enthralled me. My mother's ubiquitous charm, my father's artful dignity – they enthralled me.

Monster says: Your mother didn't love you enough to want you less than perfect.

Monster says: Your father didn't love you enough to prefer you to his depression.

Monster says: You've worked hard, you've left your mark. Maybe it's time to die. You're past the prime you wasted so much of. Why don't you join your parents? Imagine their faces as you walk towards them. They'll cry out, Oh Margo, we're so happy to see you!

Then I realize that if any of this were possible – this Sunday-school afterlife – they would be furious. My mother would cry: How dare you waste your talents and achievements like this? All our work! My father would look at me in silence, unutterably disappointed by this failure of honor and character.

And they would join arms, turn their backs and walk slowly away. Holding their heads high. ■

View from the balcony of the author's flat in the Marouf neighbourhood, just north of Tahrir Square, Cairo, Egypt, 2015
Courtesy of the author

COMING HOME TO THE COUNTER-REVOLUTION

Jack Shenker

Coming home to Cairo always starts with a lie, and this time was no exception.

The price of a taxi from the airport dwindles with each stride taken past the exit doors of the baggage hall and the stale, harried officers who guard them; those nabbed by touts at the outset pay top dollar for a limousine service that features no limousines, while the real bargains are to be found out beyond the terminal building where the air is coarse and mucky and the night slams up hot against your skin. You need a bit of guile to get there, though. My usual tactic is to chatter animatedly to no one on my mobile; I try and put on a real ensemble performance, all phatic fakery and apologetic grimaces to anyone who endeavours to catch my attention along the way. '*Ya brince!*' I yell into the void. 'I've just arrived, bring the car round!' Sometimes I pile on so much comradely slang in an effort to sound authentic that I get tangled up and trip over my words, momentarily confused by the silence at the other end of the phone.

On this occasion, the aged Peugeot I ended up in was parked on a far-flung traffic island on the fringes of the airport, wedged between a rubbish bin and an ornamental tree. The exterior was reassuringly scratched and bruised, and its dashboard was covered in plastic fruit and prayer beads and ornate tissue boxes crowned with nodding dogs shrink-wrapped in velour. Its front-left tyre had come to rest on a hunk of rubble, leaving the vehicle sitting at an erratic angle from the ground, swaying slightly in the gloom. The driver made me wait so that he could execute a synchronised shove down on the bonnet and prevent the whole thing tipping over as I climbed in. He said he was sorry for the inconvenience. But of course these are the days when everything in Egypt is at an angle: nearly familiar, yet one step removed.

Large fragments of plaster were scattered on the dusty floor of my flat. Looking up, I realised they came from the kitchen and bathroom walls. The municipality had been promising to bring piped gas to our street for years, and drive the *embooba* ('gas canister') vendors – who strap four cylinders at a time to their tottering bicycles and smack them with spanners at godawful hours of the morning in an effort to drum up business – out of the neighbourhood. No one thought it would ever happen, but it had and in my absence, the workmen, with no cigarettes or banter or small change to incentivise them, had understandably taken a route-one approach to installation: gouging massive holes out of the internal partitions to run pipes through to the boiler and oven, and simplifying their task further by repositioning these two appliances as close as possible to one another, which involved dragging the latter right across the kitchen door.

In the process, the electricity had been knocked out. I clambered gingerly over the oven by the light of a torch and caught sight of my old revolutionary posters, tattered a bit at the corners and stuck awkwardly out of time on the cupboards. Next to the sink was my 6 April youth movement mug, bearing the clenched-fist logo of what used to be one of Egypt's leading anti-regime forces. They were subversive once, these pieces of uprising ephemera, but in a way that seemed to put you on the right side of history as it tilted. They bought you some sort of place among the chants and the marches and the kids who picked up tear-gas canisters and barrelled them back towards police lines. Then, after Hosni Mubarak fell, they became kitsch. Vendors set up stalls where you could purchase number plates and T-shirts and commemorative clocks emblazoned with protest poetry and the faces of the martyrs, and what had been a badge of honour for the self-congratulatory young and conscientious journalist became something of an ironic statement instead, up there with the Hassan Nasrallah laser pens and antique Stella beer mats dotted around people's living rooms.

And then, quicker than we ever imagined, they became dangerous. The martyrs, it turned out, had died because they were duped by a foreign plot to sow chaos in Egypt and bring bloodshed to its shores. The 6 April movement is banned now, its leader thrown behind bars soon after the coup which brought military general Abdel Fattah al-Sisi into power in July 2013. The reproduction of the clenched fist – a terrorist symbol, according to the statute books – is punishable by law. The country is engaged in 'fourth-generational warfare,' where information is the weapon and media outlets the battlefield; it has enemies everywhere, seeking to distort the state, and although some of those enemies scheme far away, with maps and tanks and uniforms at their disposal, there are others lodged far closer, right inside the citadel, and it is from their hands and their propaganda that the decisive blow, if it comes, will surely fall.

I wondered what the strangers who had entered my home had seen, and what they made of what they'd seen, and what I was to them. And I cursed myself for my carelessness. Funny how inanimate objects acquire new meaning while sitting perfectly still; how violence can steal into the mundane.

16 October 2016: Rumours are circulating that TV host Amr al-Leithy has been suspended after he aired a video of a tuk-tuk driver raging against the state, reports al-Dostour *newspaper. 'We watch the television, we find Egypt is like Vienna. We go to the streets, we find out it's like Somalia's cousin,' claimed the unnamed driver, in footage that has now gone viral and been viewed over 5 million times on the internet. 'The people are not educated, the people are tired, the people are hungry.' Meanwhile, a taxi driver has set himself on fire in Alexandria to protest his inability to afford rising prices as a result of the economic crisis, leaving him with burns on 95 per cent of his body.*

17 October: In an editorial for his newspaper, Youm7, *Dandrawy El-Hawary criticises how social media users on Facebook and Twitter elevated a tuk-tuk driver to the status of preacher, while ignoring the credibility of the most prominent Egyptian scientists who say that Egypt's situation is improving. El-Hawary described this as 'the deterioration of the concepts of all core values'. He claims that the recent viral video of a tuk-tuk driver protesting current living conditions must have been staged, arguing that it would not be possible otherwise for a tuk-tuk driver to come out with such pessimistic thoughts.*

My Cairo is an inverted city, one that wears its innards above the skin. The networks upon which life depends – flows of commerce, of infrastructure, of social relations – tend not to be buried under asphalt or packed into container trucks, but left open to the elements. Ice carts criss-cross dusty backstreet alleys and eight-lane highways, dripping trails of water. At Eid, great flocks of livestock are herded along broken pavements and into the lobbies of grand, decaying apartment buildings to slaughter. Here, the poor live on the rooftops of the rich, or are jammed in against the crash barriers of roads which carry the wealthy to gated villas in the dunes. Some occupy the tombs of the capital's old aristocrats, rigging up the resting places of the departed with satellite television and turning grave markers into shelving. When the guts of a place are as visible as this, it is easy to think of yourself as one with it during the good times, and as foreign as a virus during the bad.

In Arabic, Cairo is known as *Umm el-dunya*, the mother of the world, and it is home to more than 20 million people. 'The city is no different from any other mother,' says my friend Ziad. 'You feel safe in its arms when it loves you and totally alone when it doesn't.'

In the months after I first arrived in the Egyptian capital, nearly a decade ago – on a long-distance bus from the Sinai port town of Nuweiba, which fetched up at a suburban coach station in the early hours of a weekday morning under a sky both roseate and grey – it was through Ziad and his gang that I discovered Cairo. We sat on the rooftop where Ziad lived with his alcoholic father and gazed out west across the Nile, talking of the things you talk about when the whole world is at your feet. We smoked shisha on broken chairs amid the labyrinthine din of the *bursa* (stock exchange district) – all empty now, obviously, with the cafes long shuttered and security forces guarding the quiet at both ends – and made jokes about the terrible photos of politicians that appeared in the state newspapers. We rode out to play football matches together, in Mostafa's car if he had money for petrol and on Sami's motorbike if not. Sometimes Sami would put on a cheap pair of sunglasses for the journey and pretend to be the President. 'Make way, motherfuckers!' he'd whoop, as we darted in and out of coagulated traffic streams and I clung on to his sweaty backside for dear life. 'Very important people, coming through!'

It seemed then that Cairo was opening itself up to me with a cheerful curiosity, pushing in through the front door in the shape of the milkman, the postman and the *bikya* ('clutter') collector; yet it was also pulling me out into its circuitry on missions to track down random commodities and comforts: desk lamps, shower heads, portable heaters and hash. Every time I returned to Egypt, which was almost always at night, the first thing I did upon reaching the flat was stand for a few minutes on the balcony and stare down at the parked cars and the stray cats and the rear of the giant advertising hoardings mounted at the far end of the road, facing a busy flyover, lending the whole neighbourhood a sort of backstage thrill, and in the midst of it all I would try to pick out the bats. There were always bats, wheeling and diving across the narrow space between my towering apartment block and the next. I loved the way they seemed oblivious to the distinction between building and street, vanishing formlessly into private recesses and then bursting into the air without warning, a rapid kaleidoscope of black on black. Everything around me seemed a bit like those bats, half-in and half-out. Plastic tubes crept out of mounted air-conditioning units and wound themselves around the dusty trees which lined the street. Ropes dangled from windows carrying a *sabat* – the wicker basket through which money is passed to shopkeepers on the ground below and food loaded up in return. Bags of rubbish were chucked from higher floors, sometimes careering off a washing line as they fell and spilling open their contents into the breeze so that a mishmash of family detritus – discarded shampoo bottles, dinner leftovers, Fayrouz bottle tops, and once a black-and-white photo of two children, perhaps a brother and a sister, posing stiffly in their best clothes in the 1970s – cascaded in slow motion from one balcony to the next.

I watched a fire one night from my balcony as it raged in an adjacent block of flats. I watched verbal altercations and furious punch-ups that ended as suddenly as they began. I watched the long, monotonous laps of the elderly dog walker who lived on the floor above; the kids who got high on the steps of the industrial bank opposite and played *mahraganat* music from their mobile phones; the shoeshiner who perched on his chair alone through the dark hours, moving only to dip his head almost imperceptibly in acknowledgement of any rare passers-by. I got the shape of things, or I thought I did, but the details and their meanings were usually clouded in fog. The next morning I'd go downstairs and ask Anwar, who ran the grocery store, to bring everything into focus. In return, I helped him translate the messages he received from a Scottish woman he'd met on a sex chat website.

On my last Cairo homecoming, in the autumn of 2016, once I'd climbed off the oven and fiddled around with the fuse box for a while, I walked out onto the balcony and watched the soldiers. They stood in pairs next to their armoured vehicles, motionless, faces clad in balaclavas and automatic weapons by their sides. Every now and again one of them would peer upwards and our eyes would briefly meet, and then someone, usually me, would break away in embarrassment and look elsewhere. I'd love to ask Anwar about the soldiers, about how he feels seeing them annex our little street, about the imminent protests in the main square that the soldiers have been stationed here to disperse. I'd love to ask him whether he ever locks eyes with them too, seeking something ragged and human within their fixed postures, and about how that uncompromising detachment of the state, its helmets and metal grilles, fits in with everything else around us, with all the in-betweenness.

But Anwar is long gone; he lives in Edinburgh now, on a student visa, and his grocery store has been turned into a coffin shop. So instead I lean back against the balcony wall, light a cigarette and attempt to clear the fog myself. The shoeshine guy is sitting alone on his chair as usual, his polish and brushes gathered in a rolled-up mat at his feet. It's as if he has been there forever, impervious to upheaval. There is no sign of the bats.

19 October: 'Interior Minister asserts security apparatus is not affected by rumours intended to destabilise national security,' reads the front-page headline in the newspaper al-Dostour, *following reports that an online Facebook page entitled 'Revolution of the Poor' has initiated calls for a protest on 11 November, apparently attracting more than 100,000 supporters in a single month. 'The police, armed with the latest in cutting-edge scientific methods, are able to protect the people,' Interior Minister Magdy Abdel Ghaffar assured the public in a speech on Tuesday. The newspaper* al-Masry al-Youm *claims that the protest calls are part of an attempt by international bodies to disseminate false information and foment unrest within Egypt. Sources tell the newspaper that a large amount of money has entered Egypt from international sources to fund Muslim Brotherhood 'brigades' who run anti-regime accounts online.*

20 October: 'Sugar queues continue, as Supply Minister asserts there is no crisis,' reads the main headline in the privately owned al-Watan *newspaper. Egyptians continue to be unable to find sugar at affordable prices, despite several high-profile government officials and media outlets denying the existence of any crisis.*

A cartoon in state-owned al-Ahram *newspaper depicts a police officer detaining a citizen who, he says, 'stole a spoonful of sugar when he left the coffee shop'.*

'Do you remember the ringtones?' I ask Kamal. We're on the north-west side of Tahrir, in gridlock, me thrumming spryly on the steering wheel, him with his feet up on the dashboard, staring out at nothing through the windscreen. The ringtones were a favourite of mine: I'd be walking through one of the narrow passageways that knit this part of the city together, searching out some replacement batteries or a *mazboot* coffee or just a brisk, strobe-light pageant show of mundane Cairene bustle, and then a passing stranger's phone would clatter into life. *Yaskot, yaskot hokm el-askar*, it would sometimes sing. *Down, down with military rule*. Occasionally it was a single voice, set badly to music (the inexorable fate of all revolutionary slogans is to be set badly to music); usually, though, it would be a recording of an actual protest chant, thousands and thousands of grainy voices gathered at any one of a thousand moments of pregnant possibility, all overlaid on top of each other. Kamal gazes in my direction for a few seconds without replying, then waves his hands languidly at the vehicle fumes and resumes his original position.

Kamal has curly black hair and an unruly beard; he's in his mid-twenties and suffers from a form of PTSD. He's from Port Said originally, on the Mediterranean, but he came to Cairo when the revolution started because it was where yesterday was crumbling, and if you saw something hopeful in that crumbling then it was where you wanted to be. On the day it all began he passed out in the fighting and woke up handcuffed to a hospital bed. When he tells the story of his escape, which involves a sympathetic nurse called Amira and a botched attempt to drug the police guard and many nights spent in the torture cells of Gebel El-Ahmar, the 'Red Mountain' district of the capital where several security buildings are located, Kamal's eyes widen and vivify, and he rocks back and forth impulsively on his seat. But more often than not his eyes are slightly glazed, and they rest on the middle distance. 'The expectations we had, they didn't just disappear,' he told me once, during one of our long car journeys together. 'They became their complete opposite. It's not that our dreams didn't come true, it's that we tasted them and then they turned into the worst of nightmares. And I think that when high hopes are suppressed they become a deep sadness, because energy – you know this from physics, right? – energy never dies. It has to turn into something else, another kind of energy or action, but here there's no outlet for any of that, just a vacuum.'

We retch forward a little in the traffic, towards the site of the National Democratic Party building – the headquarters of Mubarak's ruling party, which were burned down in the uprising and later demolished by the government as part of a generalised scrub down of urban memory. It occurs to me that we are level with the spot where the second field hospital had been situated, and where the *shebab* ('youth') had once stood with colanders and loaves of bread and strips of cardboard on their heads as the rocks rained down, forming the first line of the revolution's defence. They've put up new railings now and remodelled the air vents that rise from the underground car park in front of the Nile Ritz-Carlton, so that the space is diced and bordered and will be much harder for unsanctioned crowds to ever spill into from the margins as they did before. There are the same patterns in the brick tiles, over and over; it looks like a self-generating computer landscape that could stretch to infinity, without ever being interrupted. Maybe it always looked like this, I think to myself. It's just that before there were so many people jostling on top of the tiles that you couldn't tell.

Kamal counts out the beats of his adult life by the political events which have shaped it. Comedy show X came out after rally Y, but before court decision Z. So-and-so's friend got married three weeks after this massacre; they took their honeymoon just as that sit-in was getting under way. Places and times collapse into one another, which is a messy business when you're physically navigating a metropolis while simultaneously trying to keep the ghosts of the past at bay. Mostafa Mahmoud is a street to the south-east of Tahrir, but it's also November 2011, when protesters battled to reach the interior ministry and the police resisted by blinding them with birdshot. Ittihadiya is the presidential palace in leafy Heliopolis, but it's also

December 2012 and the fierce fighting between opponents and supporters of the Muslim Brotherhood. Rabaa al-Adawiya Square is in suburban Nasr City near the stadium, but it's also August 2013 and the time Islamist demonstrators wrote the names and phone numbers of their parents on their arms so that their bodies could be identified, and the ensuing slaughter that left nearly 1,000 people dead. Kamal is not an Islamist, but he knew seven individuals who were killed at Rabaa. 'The first time I was arrested and beaten, I was nineteen,' he says matter-of-factly, when I ask him about personal milestones. 'The first time I carried a corpse, I was twenty.' We work together, me and Kamal, and I feel like everything we report on in counter-revolutionary Egypt is also a report, solipsistic and urgent, about ourselves.

Military service in Egypt is mandatory for those insufficiently moneyed or connected, and Kamal has been 'extending' a long-finished undergraduate degree for years in an effort to avoid being called up. But he can't do this indefinitely and the deadline is fast approaching; he could get out of the country and try to claim asylum in Europe, but then he wouldn't be able to return and see his mother who has hepatitis, the same disease that killed his father, and she relies on his support. So he stays and smokes weed and goes to cafes to play backgammon, because that way he can avoid talking. 'I've become a master in backgammon,' he shrugs. 'I concentrate on playing because I don't want anyone to ask, "How are you?", and because I don't want anyone to ask the next question, which is, "What happened?", or the question after that, which is, "What will you do now?" '

Every few weeks the isolation gets too much. In the aftermath of Rabaa, unable to find a common language with the large numbers of people who cheered on the state's violence, but also desperate for human contact, Kamal pretended to be interested in renting a flat and accompanied a property broker around several Cairo apartments purely so he could indulge in conversation. He chatted with landlords about utility bills and deposit arrangements and walking distances to the metro, because that was so much simpler than talking about the things he'd seen in the morgue. He describes this city, the one he came to because it promised to open every door, as an open prison. 'I'm just waiting,' he declares abruptly, as I finally managed to extricate us from the jam around Tahrir and nose our car up onto the bridge. 'I'm just waiting, and I don't know what for.'

24 October: 'Muslim Brotherhood plan to create chaos', reads the headline in al-Wafd *newspaper. According to anonymous sources, the banned Muslim Brotherhood group has been exploiting recent price hikes and shortages of sugar, baby formula and medicines to incite anger among Egyptians and mobilise them against the authorities ahead of the proposed 11 November protests. The newspaper cites a report prepared by the interior ministry's security services which reveals that the Brotherhood secretly stores large quantities of sugar in numerous governorates around the country. It adds that the group manipulates citizens' feelings by encouraging frustration concerning any government reform, by using media outlets based outside Egypt to further incite dissatisfaction, and by asking people to participate in protests to create chaos. The report accuses the Brotherhood of 'economic terrorism', a term it deems no less dangerous than armed terrorism.*

25 October: 'Sisi tells youth that challenges are great amid few resources', reads the main headline in privately owned newspaper al-Masry al-Youm.

There were raids downtown last night. A friend texted: *They've started near Hardee's, same as last time. Remember, lights off, no noise, hope that they don't force entry.* I head down the stairs to buy some candles, past the Coptic family who leave the television on all day with the door open, and the woman with the speech impediment who places water bottles on everybody's doorsteps for reasons that nobody can fathom, and the *hagga* ('older woman') who spends all her time darning in the first-floor cubbyhole. She used to have a gilt-framed portrait of Mubarak in there, tacked up above the chair. For a while she replaced it with a picture of a horse standing by a lake, and now it's a photo of Sisi. I smile and nod at each neighbour as I skip past, and they smile and nod back, and I try to retain an exact image of every smile and every nod in my mind. I want to scrutinise them later, and work out whether there is anything different about these smiles and nods, the ones proffered now amid the clampdown, compared to the smiles and nods that came before.

It's wet outside, which is a novelty. It almost never rains in Cairo, but when it does the drops are plump and satisfying. The rain washes flotsam off the street into crevices and hollows, so that every concrete fissure oozes *koshari* cartons and half-finished bags of chilli sauce. In other parts of the country, the rain has caused flooding; nearly thirty people have died, according to the newspapers, and in Ras Ghareb residents are so angry that they have shut down the main highway and blockaded the prime minister's entourage, demanding that Sisi send help. But Sisi is in Sharm El-Sheikh for a government-sponsored youth conference; more than 200 MPs are there with him, all aged over fifty. Reports are spreading on social media that several young Egyptians have walked out of a session dedicated to 'youth and social justice' because none of them were allowed to speak. On state television, a correspondent sent to cover the conference welcomes the unexpected downpours, explaining that the presence of rain indicates Sisi's project has divine support.

In the late afternoon, Kamal and I drive to Giza for an appointment with Dandrawy El-Hawary, co-founder and executive editor of *Youm7* – a punchy, popular media outlet that racks up more readers than almost any other and offers the regime full-throated support. I've been fascinated by El-Hawary for ages; of the many establishment columnists who dominate the evening papers he is usually the loudest in his outrage and the rowdiest in his conspiracy theories. He is particularly hostile to other journalists, especially foreign ones, and to lily-livered liberals who complain about police abuse, and to the country of Qatar, which is supportive of the Muslim Brotherhood, and which he is convinced has been 'exporting gays' to Egypt in an effort to encourage debauchery and the wearing of women's clothes. 'Egypt could occupy Qatar with a folk music band in just two hours,' El-Hawary claimed recently, although with the caveat that it would debase the Egyptian military to bother doing so.

Those floods upstream have disturbed the Earth and freighted the Nile with soil; the river is a ribbon of luminous mud. Outside the *Youm7* offices, security guards in black shirts pace up and down and mutter into walkie-talkies. Stage by stage, gatekeeper by gatekeeper, we enter. El-Hawary, waiting to shake each of us firmly by the hand, is wearing glasses, an expensive-looking wristwatch, and a pink, striped shirt with the words LA GRANDE MÉTROPOLE embroidered above the cuffs. 'Welcome, welcome,' he beams, leading us into a conference room. 'What coffee will you have? Obviously I can't promise any sugar!'

I wonder what El-Hawary will make of Kamal. A few weeks ago, he penned a column accusing political activists of being the willing dupes of Egypt's international enemies, and insisted that male revolutionary types were so effeminate that it was impossible to distinguish them from their female counterparts. Kamal is unshaven and wears a scruffy top; he looks like a revolutionary type because he is a revolutionary type. But El-Hawary is in a generous mood and if he does have any criticisms of Kamal's appearance then he checks the impulse to share them. 'Let me make this clear first,' he proclaims with a sort of booming geniality as we take our seats. 'I stand with the state, and with stability.'

Our drinks arrive and El-Hawary breaks off to dab at a rogue splash of coffee grounds on the Formica. 'You'll notice,' he says in a low tone, as if confiding a secret, 'that there is not a scratch in this whole building. We take care of cleanliness here.' He explains that smoking and beards and the leaving of jackets on the backs of chairs are forbidden for *Youm7* employees in the workplace. He tells us that his academic background studying Egyptology has taught him the importance of order and of things being in their right and proper place. 'We cannot afford more demonstrations, more uprisings,' he warns gravely. 'I don't understand why people keep doing this, why "human rights" has to mean protests. Because what's coming with that is ISIS.'

This love of disinfection must make Cairo unbearable for people like El-Hawary, who yearn for a more sanitised universe. The revolution left jackets on the backs of chairs and then threw chairs through the windows. But this is their moment now, El-Hawary's and his ilk, and maybe that is why they are building a new capital out in the eastern desert, plunging billions into wide, tidy boulevards and neatly segregated business zones while bread riots play out in the old cities left behind. I've been to the construction site, a sprawling area just south of Madinat Badr, and paced across the helipads and the hotel complexes and the ceremonial mound from which Sisi will one day inaugurate the future Cairo, which is bleak and sandy and wrapped in a frayed tarpaulin. The regime believes in a binary choice, between total chaos and total control, and if current Cairo was the former then this new capital will be the anti-Cairo: purged of its itinerant shrimp sellers and its outdoor mattress stitchers and its pairs of lovers holding clandestine hands while crouched in the scummy, piss-stained underbelly of the 15 May Bridge. There will be no place in the new capital for white bed sheets strung up between lamp posts by rebellious teenagers and pressed into use as makeshift cinema screens, projectors powered by hacked electricity boxes to broadcast illicit footage of army atrocities to the streets. There will be no audience for the bed sheets, because the new capital will be the antithesis of density and anyway the lamp posts will be too far apart. I spoke to an engineer out there who told me that the state's synthetic new home will boast the second biggest dancing fountain in the world, and I didn't know what to say. Afterwards, I met a group of dust-streaked labourers who were helping to build a wall which will eventually encircle the whole city, insulating it and its inhabitants – the first of whom will be Egypt's government ministries – from all those jackets on chairs and spilt coffee grounds; from the smoking and the beards and the rest of recent history's unpalatable debris.

An urban planning expert described the new capital to me as a bad version of *The Truman Show*, but up close it looked more confused and menacing than that, more like an attempt to draw a line under an unfinished story, but one that just falls short. The section of the wall that the labourers were working on reminded me of a medieval fortress, massive and unyielding. One of them unzipped his trousers and urinated on it. 'This town is for the happy people, the ones who fly above us,' he said.

I asked El-Hawary whether he saw me as a direct and deliberate conspirator against the Egyptian state, and with a polite and concerned paternalism he assured me that he did. I asked him who was employing me and orchestrating this conspiracy, and he mentioned Hillary Clinton, Qatar, MI6, the *Guardian*, the *Daily Mail* and the BBC. There didn't seem to be much left to discuss after that, so we exchanged some more pleasantries and he led us out of the conference room, conducting a tour of the office artwork on the way back to the lifts. The corridors were lined with large colour-saturated photographs: a simple man in a traditional *gallabeya*, a soldier with a single tear rolling down his cheek, a bird's-eye shot of the 25 January 2011 protests in Tahrir that unseated Mubarak, with huge Egyptian flags being held aloft by the crowds, and a studio close-up of Angelina Jolie. It was a roller coaster ride through the regime's schizophrenic subconscious, and every single frame was mounted flawlessly to its wall. 'The authorities have made up their minds: meaning is dangerous, defending it is a crime, and its advocates are the enemy,' wrote leading revolutionary Alaa Abd El Fattah this year, from his prison cell. 'Once we were present, then we were defeated, and meaning was defeated with us.'

27 October: 'Sisi urges media to report truth: "Media unintentionally harm Egypt and will be held accountable before God,"' reads the front-page headline in al-Dostour. *The state-owned* al-Ahram *newspaper quotes President Sisi as saying that there are organised efforts to reduce Egyptians' support for the government, arguing that Egypt's current spate of economic woes – from the devaluation of the Egyptian pound to increases in the price of basic commodities and market fluctuations – are part of a deliberate ploy aimed at demolishing the country.*

3 November: 'Pre-emptive strikes against terrorist chaos prior to 11 November,' reads the headline in Youm7. *The newspaper reports that following the issuing of arrest warrants for several Muslim Brotherhood members on the charge of spreading rumours, attempting to overthrow the government and inciting hatred, several terrorist cell members and students coerced into terrorist activity by the Muslim Brotherhood have now been apprehended.*

Mahmoud Hussein wears a green cap and a zip-up hoodie. His words rush out fast, like he's making up for lost time, but they are also measured, as if he'd used that lost time to pin them down, and his voice cracks slightly as he speaks. 'When I started meeting friends again,' he remembers, 'I would reach out and touch them, and ask: "Are you real? You're not just a letter? You're not just a photo?" '

I push my Dictaphone closer because there is a man next to us in the cafe who keeps laughing loudly and banging his cup against the table. Mahmoud and his older brother Tito both snap their heads towards him instinctively; they are always scanning the room, reading its rhythms and honing in on anything that doesn't fit. A waiter drifts over and speaks quietly to the man and the man holds up his hands to apologise and then extends the gesture to the rest of the cafe. 'Sorry for disturbing you,' he slurs in our direction. He sounds drunk, or maybe high on Tramadol. We turn back to each other and Mahmoud continues his story.

In January 2014, on the third anniversary of the start of the revolution and six months after Sisi's coup, he was stopped at a security checkpoint on the ring road. He was wearing a T-shirt with the words NATION WITHOUT TORTURE next to the outline of a stick-figure guard beating a stick-figure prisoner. The policeman at the checkpoint asked him who the stick-figure guard was supposed to be. 'It is a picture of whoever sees himself in that stick figure,' replied Mahmoud. The policeman knocked him to the floor. Mahmoud was held in detention without charge and tortured for 791 days. The irony, he tells me, was that it was his brother Tito's T-shirt that got him into all that trouble; it was originally Tito who was the real agitator, the revolutionary activist, and Mahmoud was wearing it in part because he was trying to emulate his sibling and live up to his ideals. Tito looks across at Mahmoud lovingly and protectively. At the time of his arrest, Mahmoud had just turned eighteen.

Over the past year the security services have carried out an average of nearly five forced disappearances a day, bundling citizens into cars as they buy their vegetables or dragging them from their beds while they sleep. Often it takes weeks or months for any word of their fate to reach family members: one released prisoner recalled a fellow prisoner overhearing another prisoner mention something about a kid from this town or that governorate who is locked up at Torah, or Azouli, or el-Qanater, or the Scorpion. There are an estimated 60,000 political detainees in jail, alongside all the regular criminals, and the prison system – both its formal elements and its less visible understructure, which is far larger and ranges across side chambers and half-forgotten cellars and nondescript outhouses scattered over military bases and regional security headquarters from the Aswan Dam to the sea – is groaning under the weight of them all. For more than a year, Mahmoud was held in a cell with 150 other people, the majority of them violent offenders. All of them shared a single bathroom.

'There is a social hierarchy in the cell among the prisoners, including a commander who is usually the oldest, and he takes charge of everything,' explains Mahmoud. The drunk man's phone starts ringing and he moves out of the cafe to answer it. Mahmoud pauses as he stumbles past. 'The first night I was there, the cell commander came over to me and saw that I was sick and he promised to find me a good sleeping place on the floor. He found me one right next to the garbage and said that if I didn't want it there were many others who would give anything to have this spot and that he was doing me a favour. It took me about five months to bargain my way to an upgrade.'

Since his release, Mahmoud has found it difficult hanging out with people his own age. Like Kamal, he struggles with the inanity of regular conversation, with the impossibility of integrating some articulation of his experiences into the regular flow of gossip, girls and football, and he finds once-familiar pathways through the city pockmarked with unease. He has taken to embarking on long walks with others who have lived through detention and who know something of what Islam Khalil, a sales agent in his mid-twenties who was snatched from his family home during a security raid, calls the inability to distinguish anything beyond the blindfold, not even the separation of night and day.

'They might take me one night to hang me from my hands and feet, naked. Or I might spend a long time with my hands tied to a post. Or maybe they'd take me for an electrocution session,' Khalil has said of his initial detention, before he even reached a proper cell. 'Your dream is to survive this place, to make it to prison or to the grave.'

The Egyptian artist Sara Fakhry Ismail has written of how, during the revolution, walks through Cairo became a collective performance, one in which 'physical and mental barriers surrendered to the power of numbers'. Today, one might walk the same route, but the journey is different. 'Walls, barricades and an ever-shrinking walkable public space in the heart of Cairo are this government's way of making sure that no group, no matter how big, can ever find their way into the centre again.'

Most of the people close to me haven't been subjected to the levels of violence suffered by Islam and Mahmoud, but they have also seen old walks and places disappear behind walls and fences, along with old frames of mind that not so long ago felt daringly new. The radical online news outlet *Mada Masr* recently published an article on the coping mechanisms deployed by journalists, activists, artists, human rights workers and scholars: 'For those who see themselves as connected to the revolution, but remain [in Egypt],' the piece noted, 'these are depressing times, and increasingly lonely times too, as friends and comrades leave or are imprisoned.' It posed the question: 'What do you do to get through?' Among the answers from readers were colouring books, computer games, knitting, kaleidoscopes, drinking, drugs and dancing. 'Spinning tops are very soothing and hypnotic,' one person responded. 'They're stable but also constantly moving, so give an illusion of stability.'

'Remaining', 'surviving', 'coping'; sometimes these things feel like failure, and sometimes, often at the same time, they have more in common with resistance, or even just hope. The vagaries of our own moods can be savage. Aida Seif El-Dawla, a psychiatrist and founder of Cairo's al-Nadeem Center, which works to rehabilitate victims of state violence, talks of a generational legacy of trauma; were there to be an almighty revolutionary wave tomorrow, she points out, and a utopian Egypt victoriously established, that imaginary country would still be faced with a psychological reckoning of a magnitude that is barely comprehensible. Al-Nadeem has been closed down by the authorities now, and El-Dawla is banned from travelling. Almost anybody who works in the field of human rights has personal experience of raids on their offices, of arrests, of asset freezes and of judicial inquiries. Since the Sisi era began, a new law regulating the voluntary sector has been passed with the aim, say observers, of 'erasing civil society' in Egypt: a protest law has in practice outlawed demonstrations, a terrorism law has forbidden journalists from contradicting the government's account of militant attacks and a military courts law has enabled any civilian accused of committing a crime at 'public or vital facilities' to be tried by the army. In addition to all that, emergency law – the hallmark of Mubarak's reign – is now back, allowing security forces to effectively detain any person, for any length of time, for any reason.

In an effort to guard themselves – from the weeds of the mind as much as from the clout of the state – many people who were propelled by the revolution into shared and common spaces are now beating a retreat into private bubbles. 'There is a sense of dispossession at those physical sites that were formerly markers of political identity,' says Lina Attalah, editor of *Mada Masr*, of the public squares and cafes and pavements which during the uprisings and the street clashes briefly became an extension of one's home. 'There is a sense that to do anything other than to keep your distance and avoid them would just take too much out of you. I go to work, and I go back home, and that's it.' Some got out of Cairo completely, of course, to London, New York, Milan and Berlin, but many others have merely relocated to the capital's suburbs: to Sheikh Zayed, to al-Tagammu, to pottery classes in Maadi, where there is grass on the roadside and the sky can be seen. Coping takes its toll, maybe even more so than conflict. 'Sarah Carr marked herself as safe during general everyday existence in Egypt,' posted one friend on Facebook this month, spoofing the alerts used by the social media platform during disasters. These smaller, more reserved routines are a form of protective insulation. But they can shake something out of you in their repetition, like the work of the American composer William Basinski who, in the early 2000s, attempted to transfer his magnetic tapes onto a digital format – but found that with each loop the music became unstuck and eventually disintegrated.

Mahmoud has been forced to remake a home for himself time and again over the past two and a half years, from cell to cell, nook to cranny; where he could get away with it, he pinned up photos of loved ones on the prison walls and took up drawing to pass the time and help stave off despair. 'I liked the fact that there was no room for compliments or flattery in the cells,' he says when I ask him if anything good came out of his time there. 'There is no space for anyone to say, "Do you know who my father is?" Now I can understand people better.' The transition we make from adolescence to adulthood is always sinuous and slippery; for Mahmoud, it took place by the garbage, with 150 other people around him on the floor. 'People are confused now because the child isn't there any more,' he says. The drunk man pushes past us again, only this time, as he does so, he also seems to linger.

We exchange glances and then Tito and I make a show of calling for the bill and tussling over who will pay. There is an oud playing through the cafe's speakers and a distant hiss from a kettle and Tito and Mahmoud are texting one another and also a contact, confirming their location, warning of possible danger. They do it casually, like bored millennials, but the drunk man is watching us now and he doesn't seem drunk any more. We get ready to leave but he stands up before us and hastens towards the exit, speaking quickly and clearly into his mobile phone. We're seconds behind him and can hear a few of his words: he's reporting in to someone at Qasr al-Aini police station, which is nearby, and he's describing our physical appearance. We hurry past him and break into a trot around the corner – no faster than that because Mahmoud is on crutches, a legacy of his incarceration – and Tito, who knows the owners of the cafe, calls them as we pick up the pace and advises them that trouble might be approaching.

We weave and writhe through the murk of Garden City, which droops with mottled gates and wilting villas, bound in that moment by mutual risk and yet also poles apart – only one of us protected by his passport and the colour of his skin. And then, having made certain that the informant is not following us, we hug and depart, in separate directions.

7 November: In an editorial published by his newspaper, Youm7, *entitled 'Owners of fancy palaces object to fuel price increase and call for a revolution of the hungry', Dandrawy El-Hawary claims that all individuals criticising the government and decrying the situation of the poor – from business people and media professionals to activists – are millionaires who benefit from the chaos. Ahead of the planned protests on 11 November, El-Hawary concludes that revolutions make the rich richer and the poor poorer, and that the invention of fuel, electricity and security crises comes at the expense of Egypt's underprivileged.*

9 November: Assiut University Hospital has postponed scheduled medical operations due to a lack of anaesthesia and other medical supplies, reports al-Bawaba. *Sources tell the newspaper that more than thirty operations have been put on hold indefinitely, while fifty non-urgent medical procedures have been postponed for several months. The hospital is continuing to try and treat patients in critical condition.*

A woman tried to throw herself from the advertising hoardings at the end of my street this morning. She stood on the precipice for a long time while the traffic stopped below and a policeman tried to talk to her through a megaphone. For a long time I didn't realise what was happening: I saw the commotion at ground level, but didn't pick out the solitary figure above, still and scared, as if she had no idea how she'd got there, scrawny against the clouds. Ibrahim, the doorman of my building, told me later that apparently the woman had lost her savings in the currency crash and was demanding that someone, anyone, find her a job. Eventually, she was persuaded down and led away. She wasn't from round here, Ibrahim added, with a hint of pride.

10 November: 'Security forces arrest terrorist members of Muslim Brotherhood cells and confiscate explosives', reads the front-page headline of state-owned al-Ahram *newspaper, on the eve of major planned protests against the government. Several newspapers report erroneously that the Facebook page calling for a 'Revolution of the Poor' on 11 November has been shut down, and calls to revolt withdrawn.* Al-Wafd *newspaper claims that this 'cancellation' follows the election of Donald Trump in the United States on Tuesday, providing further confirmation that outgoing American President Barack Obama is a supporter of the Muslim Brotherhood and that Trump's rival Hillary Clinton was the main financial backer of the protests.*

In other news, the state-run National Council for Women has launched a nationwide 'Support your country, for tomorrow you get the bounty' initiative, reports Youm7. *The door-to-door campaign aims to raise awareness among women about the importance of supporting Egypt during the present economic difficulties.*

The low buildings in which the migrants hide are surrounded by reeds. They are storehouses used by the trawlers and local farmers; sometimes loaded with human beings, sometimes with grain or fish. The smugglers use code words on their radio systems to trick the navy. Bearings, times and numbers are swapped around, so two boats heading north by north-east at one o'clock might mean one boat heading west at two. Cigarettes, or *mo'assel* – the syrupy tobacco smoked in water pipes – stand in for people. The boat captains have memorised everything, Hamdy tells me. They and they alone know the vocabulary and the grammar of the sea.

I'm driving through the reeds and Hamdy is directing me, recounting the ruses he and his colleagues have used to bootleg sugar into the country over the past few weeks, and making wisecracks about Sisi. The president just gave a speech emphasising the personal sacrifices that all Egyptians must make on the road to a better future and offered his own life story as an example: he once spent ten years of his youth, he divulged, with nothing but water in his fridge. Sisi seems to have forgotten that fridges were a luxury when he was young and that even when they became commonplace only the highly privileged could ever afford to rely on permanent takeaways or a personal chef. 'Poor Sisi,' smirks Hamdy, who has a grizzled face. 'If even he is that poor, no wonder everyone else is trying to escape.'

Hamdy facilitates escapes. He is a retailer of new lives on distant shores and at the moment his product is in great demand. There are many like him up here, on the crest of the Nile at Rashid. In September, one of the migrant boats – not Hamdy's, but he knows the guy responsible – capsized just off the coast because it was overloaded, and more than 200 died. 'If young people travel behind their parents' backs, or without their parents' permission, then it is their own fault what happens and they do not deserve sympathy,' stated one parliamentarian soon afterwards. The authorities made a lot of noise about their rescue efforts, but Hamdy says that the police vessels didn't retrieve a single body from the water, alive or dead; it was Rashid's fishermen – most of whom, like Hamdy, are embroiled in the smuggling trade themselves – who brought the victims onto dry land. 'The government is the last thing we think about when we think about the valuing of human souls,' mutters Hamdy philosophically, although he knows that the same could be said about himself.

But maybe 'victim' isn't quite the right word; maybe it warps something that matters and denudes migrants of their agency.

'Almost no one thinks about the migrant until he or she becomes a lost migrant, a dead migrant, a deported migrant or an imprisoned migrant,' wrote Lina Attalah, following the tragedy. She went on to draw a parallel between the courage required to risk riding the sea with the courage required to risk joining a protest – a leap into the unknown that can likewise result in incarceration or death. Both, she points out, involve the pursuit of liberty and dignity through disruption, through revolution, through 'the kind of risk where one's entire being, body and soul, are summoned for the adventure'. That is not to say that all migrants approach their boat passage with such a mindset, nor to romanticise the horrors of the journey. But it is true that if you walk down the central strip of any number of villages around Rashid and pause in front of the larger, fancier houses, residents will tell you with some esteem about the people who live in them, and the relative of theirs who already made it to Syracuse, to Lampedusa, to Malta and beyond. It isn't hard to see why a young person with more than water in their fridge, even aside from the unemployment and the economic crises and the cruel and systemic state repression, might fantasise, one day, of following suit.

We leave Hamdy behind and begin the long drive back to Cairo, only to be stopped and detained at a checkpoint and made to wait for a state security officer from the regional headquarters to arrive and interrogate us about our movements. The soldiers are friendly and apologetic; they warm up some tea on the stovetop and pass around Kamal's cigarettes. We make big talk and then small talk and then we stand without talking for what feels like an eternity, listening to the gulls. Eventually, from the shadows, a tuk-tuk materialises wrapped in fairy lights, blaring pop and driven by a fourteen-year-old boy. It pulls up and the radio dies and a rangy, moustachioed figure emerges and immediately fills the air with barks and orders. A minute later we are back in the soldiers' hut, next to the stovetop, answering question after question about who we are and why we're here and what we think about it all. The officer notices that my surname and first name are printed in different orders on my ID document and my press card and growls the word 'conspiracy' in English under his breath. We walk the familiar high wire, probing his ego carefully as we reply so as to know when to soothe, when to placate, when to be obsequious and when to get loud and bully back, reading each other's strategies and swapping quick little glances between ourselves to ensure that each step is in tandem. The officer goes outside and radioes his colleagues and we are left listening to the gulls again and the soldiers are too scared now to make more tea. When he returns, he announces that we are free to go but that our details are being placed on record, and he issues us with a warning, although he doesn't mention what the warning is for. Then he observes, with a significant cough, that the tuk-tuk has gone and that he is twenty miles from his base. We offer to give him a lift back, because we have to, and for the next half an hour Kamal, the officer and I drive in near silence through the darkness, the wind bouncing off the storehouses and rustling through the reeds.

In the end, nothing happened on 11 November, the day upon which the 'Revolution of the Poor' was scheduled to explode. Not quite nothing, actually: there were some marches and clashes in Alexandria and Beheira and Kafr al-Duwwar and more than a hundred arrests nationwide, but in Cairo itself there really was nothing – a heavy, ersatz nothing that took the shape of long lines of police trucks at every major junction, of the special forces outside my apartment fanning out across the neighbourhood, and of no one in the streets at all. Ibrahim warned me not to step outside that day but I wanted to feel it, the nothing, and see if it unlocked the answer to a question that I didn't know how to spell out to myself or anyone else; a question that had something to do with my shifting relationship to this maddening, magical city.

I spent nearly all of my twenties here and I don't know whether it was just me, or just Cairo, or whether this is the case for everyone in their twenties wherever they might be, but it was an age when life's contours felt obligingly malleable. Now when I looked around, the ink seemed to have dried that bit more on the page. 'Each thought, each day, each life lies here as on a laboratory table,' said Walter Benjamin of early Bolshevik Moscow, and there were so many of these moments in Cairo, a whole avalanche of them, when everything was fat with imagination. I read somewhere that the colour spectrum of the mantis shrimp is four times larger than our own, and I remember wondering what a mantis shrimp might do if, having lived with all those hues, it was then made to rely on human eyes and the world suddenly appeared plainer and more predictable and more carefully, crushingly constrained. I skirted the security vehicles by taking the cut-through that runs from the back of my apartment building and down past the abandoned Italianate palace off Champollion Street, where the windows are broken and the statues chipped and the countless rooms home to no one but nesting falcons. I walked and watched and ducked into doorways to avoid passing patrols, and walked and watched some more.

And then I found Ziad, in the maze of tiny thoroughfares behind Bab el-Louq market, and he had managed to track down the only shisha place that was willing to risk opening on that asphyxiated Friday. We sat and smoked and Ziad held forth excitedly on the subject of politics and possibilities and stubborn, inchoate dreams. The next day I flew out of Egypt, just after sundown. It's the most beautiful time to rise into the air because the sky is dimmed but you can still make out the city's sparks and hollows, its many bumps and breaks. There are always kids on balconies shining lasers towards the planes as they take off from the runway, and alongside the white high beams and the orange street bulbs and the strips of green neon draped down the sides of minarets they make the earth seem restless and electric and alive. As we climbed towards the delta, I stared out of the window. Cairo looked like shattered glass, light coursing through the cracks. ■

About this time I began to suspect I was never named; people called me Mary because it was convenient, or because they had heard others call me Mary, I was in the beginning named after someone else who was named Mary but I was neither this person nor the one they called Mary after her, I was nameless, and in this state I perpetually wandered among fruit and flowers and foliage, among vines and overhanging rock and untamed animals, none of whom I could name, none of whom knew my name, nor, if they did, could they speak it. I read once that the Amazon was called the Green Hell, and if that is a name, I take it, if only as a substitute for my unknown name, which not even my parents knew when they named me Mary, after a woman who scrubbed her kitchen floor on her hands and knees, once a week, with a stiff brush. She was kind to me and I loved her, and since her death I have dreamt of her many times, either searching for her or speaking to her, but never once in my dreams have I called her Mary, which, I suspect, is not her name, or if it once was, is no longer. ■

IMAGINED MEMORIES

Francesca Todde

Introduction by Nuar Alsadir

Leaves turning to brown mulch where the gutter rises to meet the sidewalk's edge at the corner of Dorchester and 51st. The image of these leaves has, for decades, appeared in my mind in place of a thought or emotion I cannot access. Instead of a memory, my mind produces this image, which functions as a kind of recall, though I have no idea what is being called back –

The image of the leaves, I suspect, is an example of what Freud termed a 'screen memory'. Screen memories operate by a process similar to dreams, one of the tasks of which is to keep the dreamer asleep. In order for the dream not to become disturbing and wake the sleeper, according to Freud, images get split – the latent content, the powerful thought or emotion that stirs us, detaches from the manifest content, the neutral container for the emotion, which makes its way into the dream as seemingly meaningless content that rouses neither the dream censor, nor the dreamer. When successful, what he calls 'dream work' represses disturbing feelings or thoughts that might wake the sleeper while permitting the containers housing them to make their way into dreams. Memory similarly screens, or censors, powerful emotions by displacing what has the potential to be distressing or threatening with a trivial image or clip from experience that then becomes over-endowed with a vivid brightness, as with my mulching leaves.

Screen memories, however, don't offer complete repression of what might be potentially disturbing because distressing emotions may still be expressed in a mediated form that has been constructed by the mind to maximize the individual's comfort level and ability to function – a survival mechanism much like dream work, which protects sleep. The creation of a screen memory is an encoding process: the screen retains all that is important from the past, but in encrypted form. The work of psychoanalysis is to extract the meaning within the screen memory; the desires and beliefs of the unconscious that can be accessed indirectly by tracking the series of associations, displacements and elisions that went into creating the images or thoughts that the censor allowed to pass into awareness.

The street corner at which I have placed the memory of those leaves was on my walk home from school in Chicago, at the end of the block where a girl in my grade lived. Her father had drowned while they were out sailing together, and she survived. If I were to pursue the meaning packed into the image of the leaves, I would want to think about fathers and daughters, bodies of water, floating, storms, drowning, risk, loss, being engulfed. What happens if what is usually an Oedipal triangle collapses into a dyad, if a taboo fantasy is enacted in life? These are *my* spontaneous associations, which have nothing to do with the facts of the event that actually took place, the circumstances about which I know nothing.

The memories that float through our minds, that we lean on in building our personal myth, are similarly often not what happened, but what the mind has found and latched onto that allows us to screen out the thoughts, feelings and pieces of experience that unsettle us. 'It may indeed be questioned,' Freud wrote in discussing screen memories, 'whether we have any memories at all *from* our childhood: memories *relating to* our childhood may be all that we possess.' Francesca Todde's *Imagined Memories* has the quality of screen memories. The photographs show us not memories of her grandmother, but images emerging through her associations to her grandmother at the time of her death. As with screen memories, the intensity of what is in the frame, the memory image, also contains mnemic traces of that which has been kept at bay. Rather than adopting the role of an analyst trying to get at the artist's mind, the viewer of these encoded mysteries is provoked to produce his or her own associations and displacements – to use the charge of what they see on the page as a way in – not towards narrative but insight, the transcendent realm of archetypal forms. ■

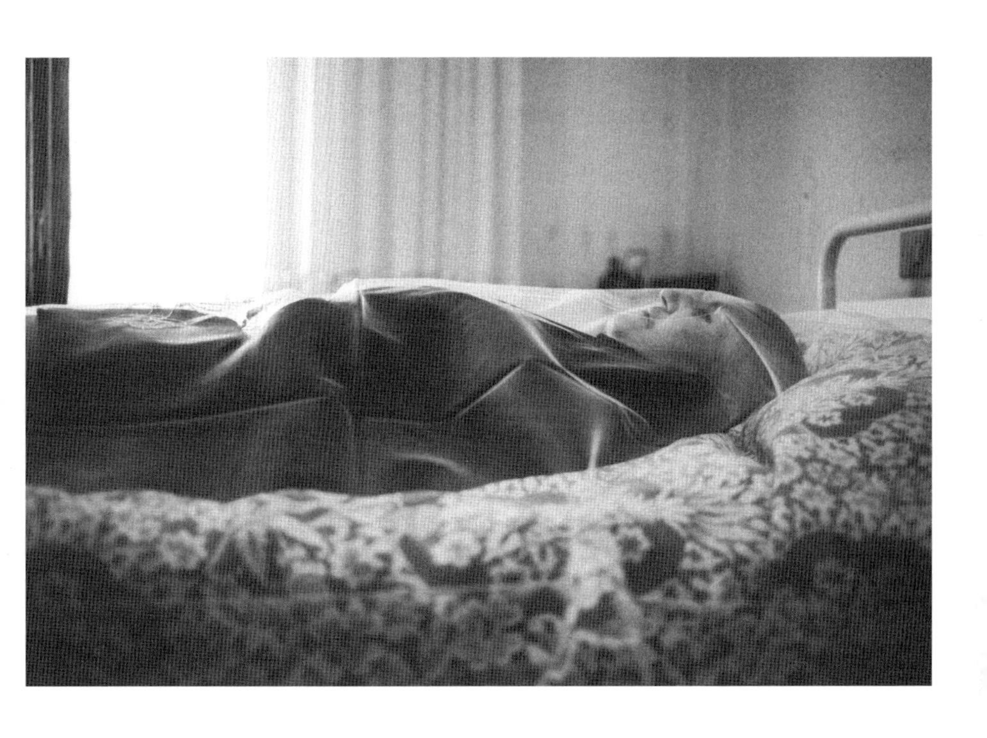

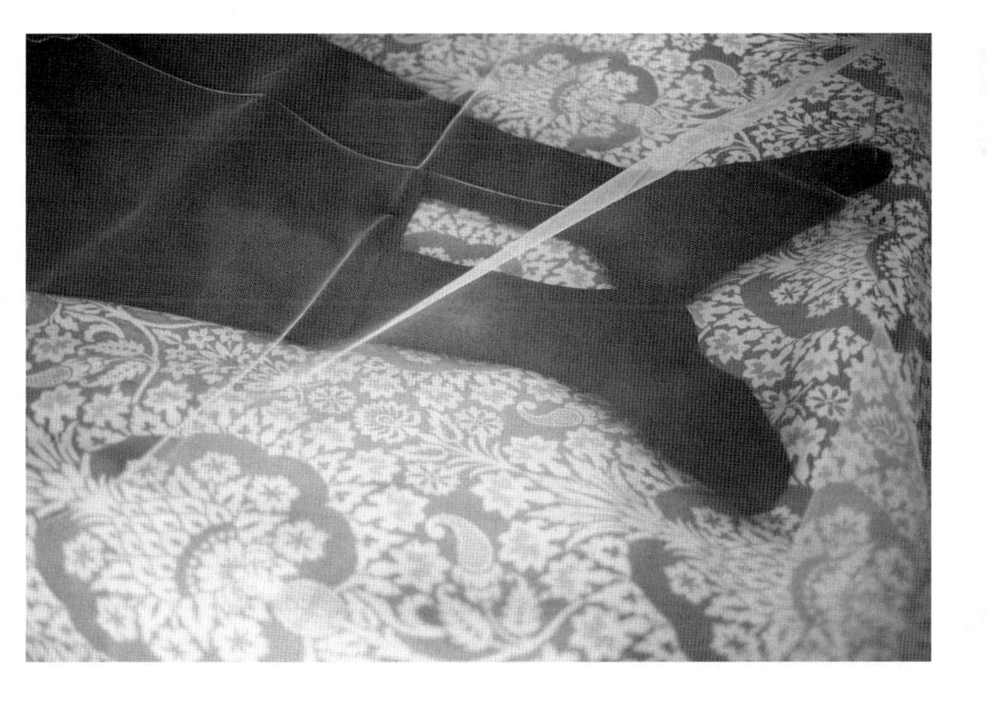

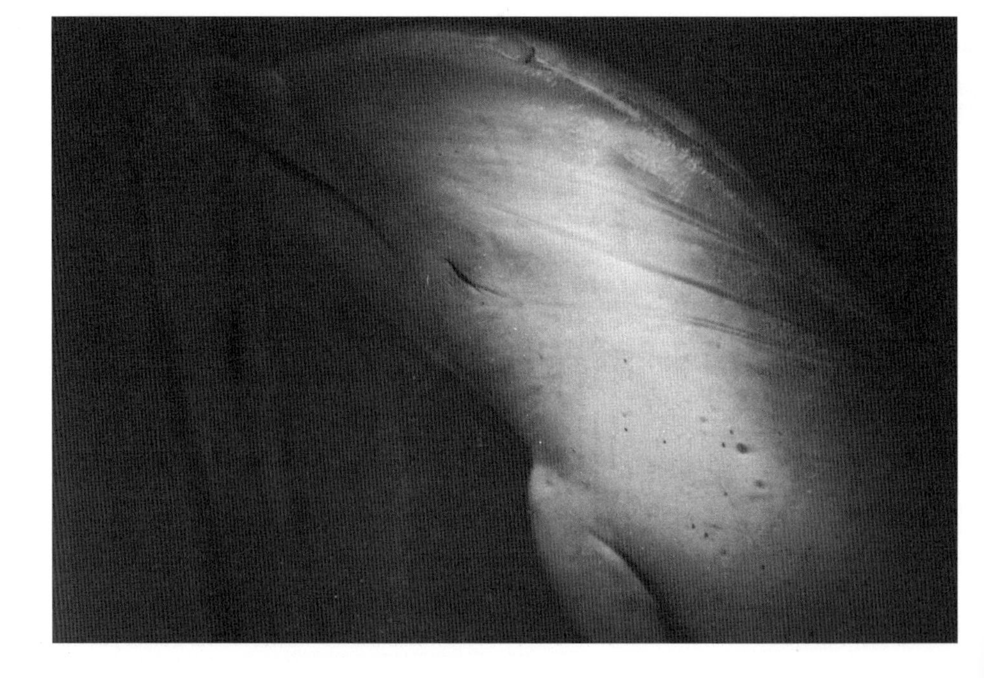

DARLING

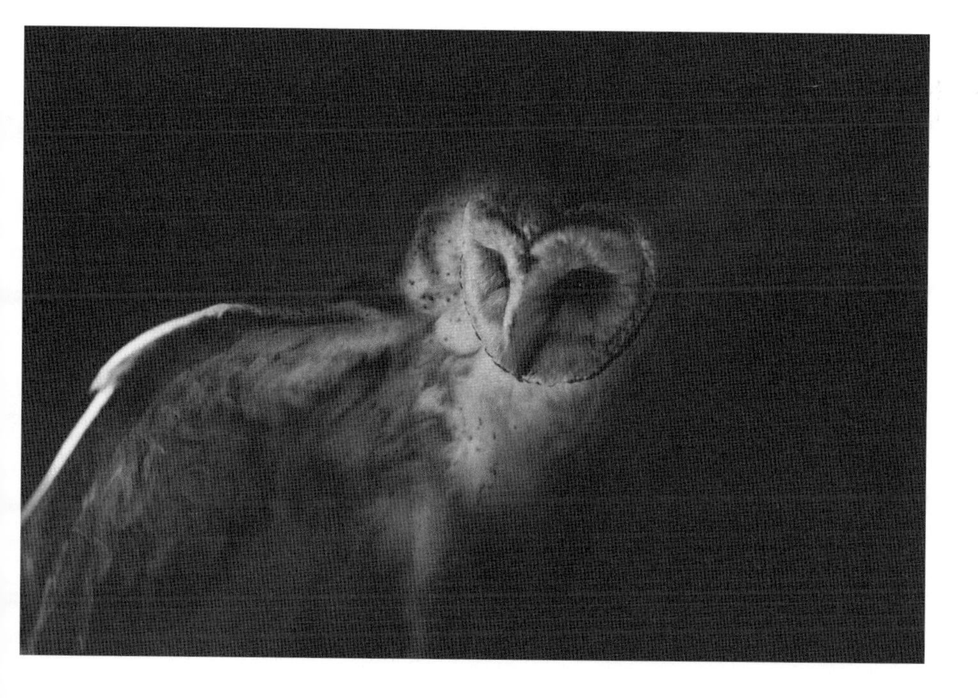

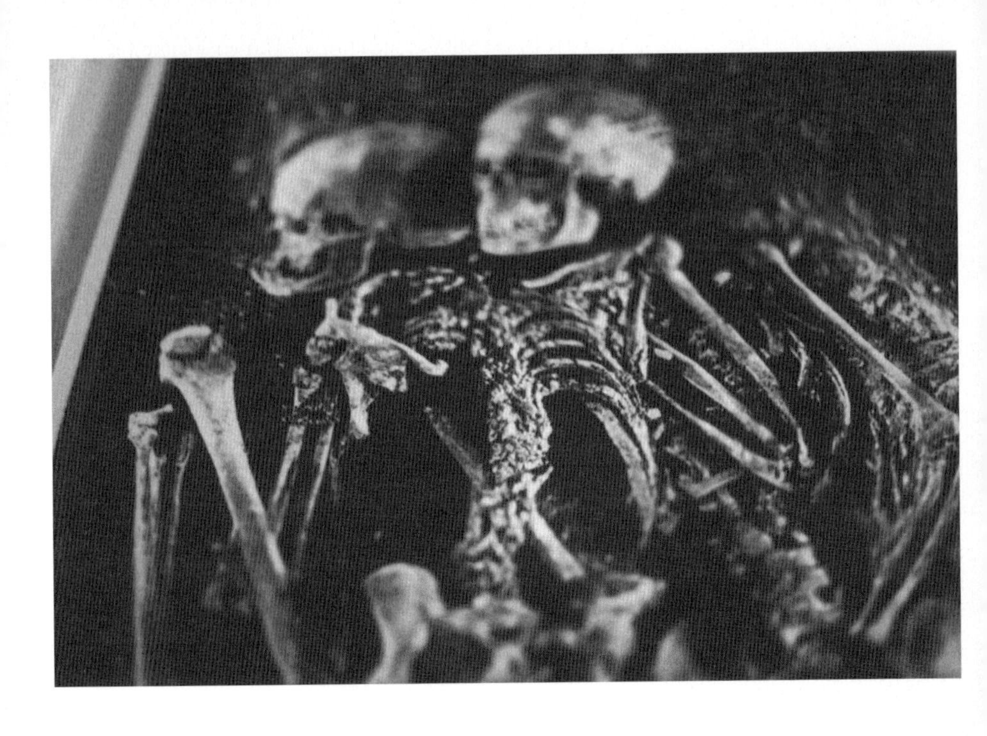